anyone but you

anyone
but
you

a novel in
two voices by
lara m.
zeises

Delacorte Press

Published by
Delacorte Press
an imprint of
Random House Children's Books
a division of Random House, Inc.
New York

Visit us on the Web! www.randomhouse.com/teens
Educators and librarians, for a variety of teaching tools, visit us at
www.randomhouse.com/teachers
Library of Congress Cataloging-in-Publication Data
Zeises, Lara M.
Anyone but you / Lara M. Zeises.
p.   cm.
Summary: Teenagers Seattle and Critter, "faux step-siblings" since
Seattle's father left her with Critter's mother six years earlier, spend
the summer sorting through their romantic feelings and making
decisions about what they want from life.
ISBN 0-385-73145-0 (trade) — ISBN 0-385-90177-1 (glb)
[1. Self-perception—Fiction. 2. Conduct of life—Fiction.
3. Stepfamilies—Fiction. 4. Brothers and sisters—Fiction.
5. Delaware—Fiction.] I. Title.
PZ7.Z3938An 2005
[Fic]—dc22   2004019879
The text of this book is set in 11.5-point Minion.
Book design by Angela Carlino
Printed in the United States of America
November 2005
10 9 8 7 6 5 4 3 2 1
BVG

For M & M, with much love and gratitude

ACKNOWLEDGMENTS

Since ninety percent of writing is rewriting, I'd pretty much be lost without the guidance of my brilliant editor, Jodi Kreitzman, who challenges me in ways an author can only hope to be challenged, and whose love and passion for the written word are apparent in everything she does. Jodi, you make me better, and you make it fun.

Many, many thanks to everyone at Random House Children's Books, including Beverly Horowitz, Kathy Dunn, Adrienne Weintraub, Angela Carlino, and Jennifer Edwards. Also to my agent, George Nicholson, without whom this project might not exist, and Paul Rodeen, who helped keep me sane even when I was half a block from crazy.

As always, I have to give mad props to the Emerson Four: Tea Benduhn, Steven Goldman, Kim Ablon Whitney, and especially Laurie Faria Stolarz, who's always *right there* when you need her, no matter what. More props to Oakland L. Childers and Lisa Whitaker, who gave me a crash course in skateboarding (no pun intended), and to Jeannie Vandover, who helped school me in All Things Rod.

I'd also like to recognize the generous support I've received from librarians, educators, and booksellers, especially those from my home state of Delaware. You've taken such good care of me, and I can't thank you enough.

Finally, I am extremely indebted to my family and friends (aka the people who manage to love me even when I morph into the Extremely Crabby Author Girl in Desperate Need of More Caffeine). Also to Christopher—when it comes to you, I can't even find the words. The best part about you, Chris, is that I don't have to, because you already *know*.

seattle

Stoopid

We were sweating out the summer on a concrete stoop, me and Critter and sometimes Jesse, swigging bottles of Coke, or maybe Bud Lights, if Layla's supply was plentiful enough that she wouldn't notice a few were missing. The central air-conditioning had broken in late May, during the first of a seemingly never-ending string of heat waves, and we were saving up to get it fixed. By "we" I mean Nurse Layla, my pseudomom, who pulled fourteen-hour shifts at the hospital, sometimes during the day and sometimes at night, because night shifts meant more money, and more money meant we'd sleep in cool rooms before September.

Jesse helped, giving Layla half the cash he earned jockeying Slushees at the Sip-n-Stop down by the Movie King. Me and Critter were supposed to pick up part-time jobs, too, but when Critter failed English (again) and I scored my own F in biology, it was no-go. For one thing, summer school started right after the Fourth of July, and no one would hire us for the few weeks we had off before our Loser Kid classes. For another, Layla wanted us studying 24/7. Getting educated, she insisted, was our real job, and if we didn't start cracking down, she'd have to start cracking skulls.

I'd thought I'd spend all my time before scholastic prison perfecting my blunt fakies at the Newport Skate Park, but another heat wave rolled into New Castle on our last day at Haley High. It was the kind of thick, wet heat that stuck to your skin like Saran Wrap and made the air wrinkle up by nine a.m. Between the extreme humidity and the hot hot sun, I was barely able to crank out a kickflip on my board before wanting to pass out.

So, we became stoop sitters. Critter, in a pair of baggy jeans that dipped low enough to show off the elastic on his optimistically large boxer briefs, and me, also in long pants of some sort, too shallow to show the neighbors the whiter-than-whiteness of my chunked-out thighs. As soon as school ended, Critter decided it was way too hot for the rumpled, smelly T-shirts he usually wore and started going shirtless, his pale, hair-less chicken chest slowly browning to the color of Mc-Nuggets. As for me, I stuck with my tank tops, even though the once-loose fabric was starting to cling to my expanding boobage.

To amuse ourselves we played whacked-out hair-stylist. Critter had me paint blond streaks into his light brown hair using Q-tips and a bottle of peroxide. Then he gelled the whole mess into bedhead spikes à la his hero, aging pop icon and legendary ladies' man Rod Stewart (no joke). We soaked my colorless hair in a vat of concentrated Berry Blue Kool-Aid, cut it chin-length, and matted the chunks into my Suburban White Girl take on dreadlocks, a feat made achievable with the aid of some unflavored gelatin we found in the pantry one day when we were raiding it for snacks.

Our days started around noon and lasted well beyond Conan O'Brien. In the mornings we'd take turns showering and breakfasting, and by the time that was all through, it was too hot to be inside and we'd land back on the stoop. If we were feeling particularly adventurous, we'd haul ass down to the Sip-n-Stop and scrounge cigarettes and Slushees off Jesse, who was convinced that we were going to get him fired, and who kicked us out after only a few minutes of air-conditioned ecstasy every single time. So we'd go next door to the Movie King, to see if Shelli was working, because she had this thing for Critter and would give us free rentals. Sometimes, if Shelli's cousin was working the same shift and could cover, Shelli would let Critter drag her behind the counter and into the back room for an impromptu groping session. He can be such the pig.

And this was pretty much the routine, until stupid me suggested that Critter use his talents to charm one of the pretty lifeguards who worked the pool at this ritzed-out condo complex across town. We'd gotten guest passes there once the summer before, when a property-developer patient of Layla's thought he could get her to go out with him if he romanced her kids first. But Layla had been like a nun since my dad walked out on us six years ago, leaving her with a broken heart, a

4

defaulted mortgage, severe credit card debt, and a then nine-year-old almost-stepdaughter (me). The property developer tried harder than most—Layla was a total babe, even when she didn't wear makeup—but ultimately bailed before we could snag more passes.

So. The pool. I'd have called it Olympic-sized but I didn't know how big an Olympic-sized pool really was. It was big, though. The shallow end alone was bigger than my bedroom. The cool blue water sloped from three to ten feet deep, where it formed the top of a T. There were two separate diving boards, the higher of which was almost twice as tall as Critter, who stood nearly six feet. You weren't allowed to jump off it unless you'd passed a diving test, and you couldn't take the diving test until you'd passed the swimming test that gave you access to the deep end. So most of our one and only visit was spent test-taking. But I didn't mind. I loved the way my body felt in water, freed from the bonds of gravity I was so conscious of when I skated. In the pool, I was like an underwater airplane, my limbs cutting through liquid like propellers.

That was pretty much all I was thinking about when I goaded Critter into seeing if he could make nice with one of the female lifeguards. That and how beautifully cold the water would be on my fry-cooker skin. I thought Critter's crooked smile could be our all-access pass to chlorinated bliss. I thought it would be fake, like with Shelli. I didn't think he'd fall in actual love.

I certainly never thought he'd fall in love with someone like *her*.

Boredom Is the Mother of Invention

We were closing in on the third week of June. Two weeks of vacation gone, just like that, and only two and a half more before we had to report to summer school. The day it hit 101 degrees, Critter and I spent the entire afternoon sitting on the kitchen floor, rubbing ice cubes over our pulse points and drinking enough water to fill one of those inflatable kiddie pools. It was this observation, which I made out loud to Critter, that gave me the idea of bluffing our way into that big mama pool from the summer before.

"No way," he said. "We'd have to take, like, four buses. And even then there's no guarantee we'd get in."

"Yes, but think how good it would feel if we did," I urged.

"Uh-uh. *No.*"

Only once I got thinking about that pool, I couldn't stop. So I bugged Critter for twelve hours straight, until he got so fed up with my nagging that he finally caved and agreed to go the following morning. I immediately started to work on Jesse—there was always strength in threes—but he refused to take the day off from work just to follow us on what he thought was a totally hare-brained scheme.

"Dude, where's your sense of adventure?" I groaned as he slipped on his Sip-n-Stop vest that sweltering morning.

"*Dude,*" he mocked. "Some of us aren't allergic to responsibility and have actual *jobs.*"

Jesse was fifteen—the same age as me—but I swore he acted like an old man. When he wasn't at work, he was usually at the homestead, *cleaning.* Not like straightening up, but vacuuming and mopping floors and polishing our furniture with orange-scented stuff. He claimed it was therapeutic, said it gave him time to think—but think about what, I don't know. Jesse kind of lived inside his own head, maybe to compensate for Critter having diarrhea of the mouth and verbalizing every single thought that crossed his hormonally charged seventeen-year-old brain.

Even though there was a bus stop a block from our house, Critter and I walked with Jesse down to the Sip-n-Stop, all loaded up with our swim stuff. While I distracted Jesse, Critter lifted us a couple of Gatorades. He tried to get Jesse to give us some smokes, too, but Jess was all, "Get a job, *Christopher*." To which Critter replied, "Later, *Jessica*." Jesse just shook his head, because after all these years, Critter still thought it was super insulting to call his little brother by a girl's name.

We walked down Route 273 a bit and waited for the number 47 bus. Fifty minutes and two transfers later, we got dumped off about half a mile from the ritzy pool place. We had to hoof it the rest of the way, which was sort of brutal, as it was all uphill and we were pretty loaded down with various bits of gear: two Walkmans, an assortment of mix tapes, tanning lotion, beach towels, PB&Js. But finally we arrived, even though we were all gross and sticky with sweat. All the more reason my body itched to plunge itself right into that clear, cold blue.

"So what's the plan again?" Critter asked as we headed toward the fence surrounding the pool.

I stopped dead. "What do you mean, '*What's the plan again?*' Critter—*you're* the plan. Remember? You."

"Yeah, I know that," he said. "But what am I supposed to do exactly? Go up to her and be like, 'Hey, baby, mind if we take a dip in your pool?' "

I sighed loudly. "No, stupid. You're supposed to *charm* her."

"What if it's not a her? Dudes lifeguard, too."

"Then lie! Tell whoever about the guy who gave us the passes and make up something about us being allowed to come here whenever."

"That sounds lame."

"You got a better idea?"

Critter stroked this imaginary patch of facial hair he kept trying to grow on his chin. "We could go to the lobby, pick a name off a mailbox, and then make like they're our grandparents or something."

"Look," I said impatiently. "Let's just stick to the original plan. We'll walk in like we own the place, and you'll tell anyone who questions us that Layla's dating that Wilson guy, and that he said we could swim here whenever. Odds are, the guard's going to be too lazy to actually check out our story, but even if she—or *he*—does, we've got one blissful swim day ahead of us. Deal?"

"Yeah, okay," he conceded. "Deal."

Swimming with the Enemy

I hated her the moment I laid eyes on her. She was everything I wasn't: long legged, lithe, poised. Her smallish boobs formed two perfect little mounds in the top of her regulation blue Speedo one-piece, the bottom of which was concealed by an artfully tied flower-print sarong. She was very tan, with the kind of smooth, even tone that comes from careful sun baking, never from a spray or one of those freaky "we'll microwave your skin for you" salons. And the hair. Shoulder-length, light brown with sun-kissed streaks of blond, flawlessly straight and topped with a perfectly chic fringe of bangs that blew around in the wind.

When we walked through the gate, we found her scooping stray leaves off the surface of the water with one of those enormous nets. For some unknown reason, the pool was completely deserted, and I think we surprised her a bit. "Can I help you?" she asked.

"We're just here for a swim, thanks," Critter said.

"Can I see your badges?" She asked this plainly, like "I'm not a bitch, just doing my job," but the sweet tang of her voice made me dislike her even more.

"Badges?" Critter asked, staring blankly at Ms. Pool Goddess.

I elbowed Critter, but there seemed to be a breakdown between his brain and his mouth. Where was his inner snake charmer? He gave me a sheepish shrug. Disgusted, I stepped in. "The guy who developed this place? He's our mom's fiancé. He said we could swim here whenever we want."

"That's weird," she said. "The guy who developed this place happens to be the father of my boyfriend, and I know for a fact that he's happily married already."

I could feel sharp claws trying to poke out my fingertips, even as my stomach began churning like I'd just chugged rancid buttermilk.

"Busted!" Critter laughed heartily. "Look, here's the deal. The guy we're talking about—Paul Wilson?—he had this thing for our mom last year and gave us some guest passes. They broke up, but she"—he thrust his thumb in my direction—"fell in love with this place. So we thought we'd try to come back for a day or two. You know, just until this heat wave breaks."

She dropped her big net on the concrete and walked closer to us, wiping her hands on her floral-print butt. Then she extended one to Critter. "I'm Sarah," she said in a soft but steady tone. "I know

Paulie. He's my boyfriend's uncle—the younger brother of the developer. Doesn't surprise me he'd try to use this pool as leverage. It's fantastic."

"I like to swim," I said, out of nowhere. My cheeks flamed from embarrassment.

"Yeah?" Sarah said. "Me too."

Critter cut in, smooth as sandpaper: "So should we leave or what?"

Sarah sucked on her bottom lip. "I don't know," she said. "Some of the people who live here are just waiting for a reason to start screaming at management. But the pool's been so abandoned lately—it's mostly old folks, and this weather's too much for them. Anyway, I don't see why you guys couldn't stay for a little while."

She smiled at me, sort of shyly, and held out her hand. I noticed immediately that her fingernails were perfect, too—a half inch long, clean, and coated with a pink and white French manicure. Her little pearl-shaped toenails, visible through her flip-flops, were painted to match.

"I'm Seattle," I said crisply. "And this dumb-ass to my right is my almost-brother Critter. It's okay, then? We can just dive right in?"

Sarah nodded. "Yeah, go ahead."

Critter cocked his head. "So how long have you been working here?"

"Just this summer," she replied. "Since Memorial Day."

"Cool, cool."

He started asking her more questions, like where did she live (Penn Acres) and where did she go to school (New Castle Baptist, which sits about two hundred yards from our own Haley High). As I unloaded my bag onto one of the lounge chairs, I tried to figure out if he was solidifying a summer pass for us or if he really wanted to know what this chick was all about. I was hoping—praying—it was the former, because, man, out of all the girls Critter could snag, *this* would be the one I could stomach the least. I mean, even Shelli would be better than this babe.

By the time I'd gotten all situated and stripped down to my suit—a black old-lady one-piece that covered as much skin as possible without making me look like a prude—Critter and Miss Thang were firmly entrenched in conversation. So I just marched up to the high dive—half stomping, actually—took a few practice bounces, and then jumped, arching my body the way my dad had taught me years ago, when he was still

13

interested in being a dad. My arms broke the water in a clean slice, and I didn't even mind the bracing cold. I pushed myself to the bottom, touched with one hand, then shot back to the surface. Critter was clapping when my head emerged. "Way to be, way to be!"

"Yeah," Sarah said. "That was awesome."

Ignoring her, I shouted to Critter, "Are you getting in or what?"

"In a minute."

I splashed away from them and decided to do some laps. I was never great at the crawl, so I mostly breast-stroked my way back and forth, breaking into brief stints of the butterfly every now and then, just to show off a bit. My fingers were all pruney by the time Critter did a running cannonball into the deep end, sending splatters of water across the hot dry concrete. Sarah giggled before retreating to her lifeguard chair. I treaded water as I watched her pull a bottle of Copper-tone from her L.L. Bean backpack, hunter green with her initials stitched along the top flap. Slowly, carefully, she squirted the white cream in a line down her long leg and very deliberately began rubbing it into her skin in small circles. I wouldn't have thought twice about this, except that *she was staring at Critter the whole damned*

14

time. I wondered how long it would be before she asked him to rub the lotion on her back.

Just then I was yanked underwater—Critter's signal that he was finally ready to play. Only I wasn't quite prepared, so my nose and mouth filled up with chlorine, leaving me sputtering and breathless once I made my way back to the surface.

"Wuss!" Critter yelled, slamming his arms into the water to send tidal waves my way.

"You're dead!" I screamed. I dove back into the water and ran into his stomach so hard that we ended up pressed against the side of the pool. When I came up for air, I could see that Sarah was frowning at how close Critter and I were to each other. I wanted to mess with her, so I threw my arms around his neck, and my legs around his waist, and shouted, "Reverse piggyback!" Critter, oblivious to my little power play, obliged me, hulking around the pool with me firmly attached to his front, my damned boobs bouncing around like two Lycra-coated buoys.

When I caught another glimpse of her, I saw that Sarah was still spreading lotion over her naked limbs, and the next thing I knew, Critter had this enormous hard-on. It startled me so much that I immediately let go of him and turned to swim away. In my haste I smacked into the water, snorting more chlorine through my nose.

As I dragged my body up the concrete steps, all I could think was *What the hell?* Critter and I wrestled all the time and not once had his boy parts tried to get freaky-friendly with my girl ones. Then a voice said, *This is Critter we're talking about. The walking hormone. The boy who once professed to getting a boner while watching Martha Stewart oil an antique coatrack. He was probably all juiced from watching the princess grease herself up.* I did my best to shrug off the weirdness, grabbed my towel, and began to dry off.

Critter swam to the ledge by me and said, "What's the matter? You okay?"

"I'm tired," I lied. "I need a break."

He nodded like he had expected me to say something to that effect. Then he dove under and swam to Sarah's side of the pool.

I spread my ratty Mr. Bubble beach towel over the length of a vinyl chaise and lay on it at a 170-degree angle—low enough to be comfortable, but high enough that I could keep an eye on Critter. My tummy bulged out a bit, so I grabbed my T-shirt and arranged it over the mound and the tops of my marshmallow thighs. I couldn't hear what Critter and Sarah were talking about, but whatever he was saying was making her laugh and toss her hair. I tried to focus on the possibility of season pool passes to get my mind off the other stuff—Sarah and her French-manicured toenails, Critter and his unexpected hard-on, Jesse and his goddamned morals. If *he* had come with us, Critter would've behaved himself better. Jess had that kind of effect on people.

The moisture on my skin shrunk into tiny tight beads before evaporating altogether. I closed my eyes, felt the fireball sun roasting my lids. The sound of my breathing mixed with the hum of the pool filter, and before I knew it, I was out cold.

critter

Hot Legs

The girl was fine. She was finer than fine—she was slamming, banging, busting, hott with-two-*t*'s supa-fine. I wasn't sure which I liked more, the long honey hair or the long honey legs. Everything about her made me think of beach sand in the late afternoon, and man, I wanted to sink right in.

"So you got a boyfriend." A statement, not a question, since she'd already mentioned him four times in the brief hour we'd known each other.

Sarah nodded. "Duncan Mackenzie? He goes to Haley—maybe you know him?"

I wanted to laugh. Sure, I knew Duncan. Knew *of* him, at least. He was one of those guys who walked the halls like they were gods—like everyone else on the planet existed solely to make them look good, even their fellow jock boys, who always walked half a step behind. In school I tried to steer clear of guys like that, Abercrombie wannabes who used "partay" as a verb and spent their weekends drinking themselves stupid.

"I've seen him around," I said. "Been together long?"

"With Duncan?" A wrinkle formed between her eyes as she ticked the time off on her fingertips. "It's about eight months now."

"Whoa," I said. "That *is* long."

She shrugged. "Yeah, I guess."

There were a bunch of thoughts bouncing around in my head. Like the idea that she and Duncan the Great were probably doing it, because no way would a guy like him wait more than three months for a piece of action. Even so, I noticed that despite frequent references to a boyfriend, when she actually said his name it was without emotion. Like he was just some guy, and not *her* guy. Then there was the fact that she'd had to count up the months they'd been together, instead of knowing off the top of her head. Officially she might be "taken," but unofficially I still had a chance.

"So where is Boyfriend now?" I asked, squinting into the sun.

"Gone," she said.

My head snapped back down. "Gone?"

"Soccer camp," she explained. "He's in North Carolina until mid-August."

"That's, like, the whole summer."

"Tell me about it."

So *that* was the source of tension. Boyfriend chooses ball over babe. Of course she was pissed. I wondered if Dunky knew that his dumb-ass decision would leave the door wide open for some other dude to sneak in and snatch his honey. It was an opportunity I couldn't pass up.

"That sucks," I said. "Isn't summer all about taking your girl down to Rehoboth? Playing mini-golf? Buying her frozen custard, kissing her while her mouth's still cold?"

She shivered. At least, I think she did. Hard to tell, because almost immediately after, she popped up from her chair, told me she needed to check the pool's pH levels, and scampered off.

I was so *in*.

No Holding Back

When Sarah returned, she slowly untied the flowery scarf thing from around her waist and draped it over the back of her chair. More leg, every inch perfectly smooth, perfectly golden. As she rubbed the thick, creamy Coppertone into her now exposed thigh, she said, "What about you? You have a girlfriend?" She said it in a practiced-casual sort of way. I took this as a sign.

"Not really," I said. "There's a girl I see, but I wouldn't call her my girlfriend." I wasn't sure if I could call what Shelli and I did "seeing" each other, but the part about her not being my girlfriend was certainly true. Far as I knew, no one had ever claimed Shelli—at least not publicly.

"So you're one of *those* guys," Sarah said, a half smile playing on her cherry lips.

I closed my eyes and shook my head. No way was I letting this kitten think I was some kind of player. "It's not what you think. I just don't believe in being some-one's boyfriend unless I'm, you know, *devoted* to them." My eyes stayed focused on her mouth. "It's hard finding a girl worthy of such devotion."

There it was again. The shiver. Only this time it was more like a little squirm. She was making me so hot. *Too* hot. I was hoping another dip in the pool might cure that problem, even though it hadn't the first time around. The little guy had a mind of his own. I told Sarah I needed to cool off.

"No doubt," she said. "I'm feeling kind of hot myself."

I grinned as I cannonballed back into the deep end. This girl was prime for the picking. I did a victory lap and splashed around for a bit, but swimming alone was mostly boring. "You should come in!" I called out to Sarah, since Sea was still snoozing. "The water feels fantastic."

"I'm sure," she said. "But it's kind of against the rules."

"Can you sit on the edge at least?"

She looked around like someone was monitoring her every move. Then she stepped out of her flip-flops and said, "Maybe for a bit."

I propped my elbows on the hot concrete not six inches from where she sat. Those legs were dangerously close to my body, and I had to fight the impulse to grab them and pull her in. I couldn't stop thinking about what it would feel like to have her sleek, wet bathing suit pressed against my naked chest, and—

"Critter?"

"Huh?"

"I was saying, your sister seems nice."

"Yeah, Sea's pretty cool. What about you? Any siblings?"

"One," she said. "Younger brother."

"Me too. Jesse's fifteen, same as Sea."

Sarah cocked her head. "Are they twins?"

"Nah, Seattle's not our real sister. Her dad and my mom got together when we were little kids, though, so she may as well be."

"So now you're one big happy blended family?"

I laughed. "Not exactly. Frank—that's Sea's dad—he's been out of the picture a long time now. Sea's mom died giving birth—this freaky blood clot thing in her brain—so really Layla, my mom, is the only mom she's ever known."

"I don't understand," Sarah said. "Her dad and your mom got divorced—and the stepmother got custody?"

"More like they never got married to begin with and old Frankie didn't exactly invite Sea along when he ran off."

23

"Oh."

"Yeah."

Whatever sexiness building between us suddenly evaporated in the stink of my family laundry. I didn't know why I'd spilled it all out to her, especially since none of us—Layla included—ever bothered to clarify Seattle's relationship to the family. She was always Layla's daughter and our sister, end of story.

I decided to shift gears. "What about you? What's your situation like?"

"Boring. Just me and my brother, parents married twenty years, blah blah blah." She looked at her feet, but I could see that her pink cheeks got pinker, like she was embarrassed.

To rescue the conversation, I hoisted myself out of the water and onto the ledge next to her, shaking my shaggy hair and spraying water all over her shoulders.

"Quit it," she said, laughing.

"Only if you say please."

"Please!"

The sun was starting to hang lower and I knew that Sea and I should be heading home soon. I got to my feet and offered Sarah my hand. She took it, looking up at me with her big blue eyes. I was a little too eager helping her up and she tripped into me, the front of her suit grazing my chest for a fraction of a second. She giggled as my blood pulsed in places I wished it wouldn't.

She put her hand behind her neck and pulled all of her hair onto one shoulder. Her lips were shining. They smelled like strawberries, and I was dying for a taste. I wondered what she'd do if I tried to kiss her.

Then a stray cloud sailed in from nowhere, covering the sun, and the moment was lost. Sarah returned to her chair and I watched the space where she'd been, like I could actually see some of her strawberry essence lingering behind.

Sweet Jesus, I thought, swallowing hard. *This girl could break my heart into a million pieces.*

seattle

Fo' Sizzle

When I came to, the sun was starting to set. I guessed it was maybe four or five. I blinked a few times, trying to remember where I was, not sure why I had a stinging sensation every time I opened and closed my eyes. The pool glistened in front of me, and on the other side of the water lay my faux brother, stretched out on his own vinyl chaise, back facing the sky and head tucked on his hands. I thought he was still talking to Sarah, but his eyes were closed. I hoped conversation was involved, because otherwise, she was just sitting there watching him sleep, and that was way too creepy.

I tried to sit up but was nearly blinded by pain. I looked down at my formerly eyeball white skin—skin that had, during my impromptu nap, turned the bright red of a cooked lobster's shell. Everything hurt. *Everything.* I moved the T-shirt that had been covering my paunch and discovered, to my great horror, that I now had a strange tan line mid-thigh. The tops looked like a cheerleading skirt made of paste-colored cellulite. It looked particularly sickly when paired against the scarlet that covered the rest of my bod.

I stood up, wrapping my towel around my waist like a low-rent version of Sarah's flowered sarong, and made my way toward Critter in mincing steps. When I got to him, I lifted my foot and jabbed it into his knee pit. "Why'd you let me sleep like that? I'm all burned up."

Critter rolled over lazily, took one look at me, and started to laugh. "Dude, you're a cherry tomato!"

"I know," I snapped. "Didn't you see me frying out there? Or were you too busy making nice with our new friend to notice?" I said that last sentence in a lower tone, but still loudly enough that Miss Sarah could hear me.

"Chill, mama," Critter said. "You're just cranky because you didn't have your lunch. Go raise that blood sugar level and morph back into the sweetie girl I know and love."

"Piss off. I'm going home."

I strode back to the other side of the pool, where all my stuff was. I couldn't believe that Critter would talk like that to me, especially in front of *her*.

Gently, I pulled my T-shirt over my head and stepped into my khaki pants. Every time the cloth brushed against my skin, I ached. I had no idea how I was going to make the long trek back to the bus stop, let alone make all those transfers and haul ass back up the hill to our house.

"Um, Seattle?" It was Sarah, looking timid. "The pool closes in five minutes. . . . If you guys don't mind sticking around while I finish up, I can give you a ride home."

"Nah—wouldn't want to put you out or anything."

"I wouldn't have offered if I didn't want to do it."

"We'd love to catch a ride with you," Critter said, sidling up to us. "Right, Sea?"

"Whatever."

She drove—what else?—a beige BMW. It was a slightly older model, but in pristine condition nonetheless. A crystal heart hung from the rearview mirror. *Gag.* I sighed heavily, sank deep into the butter leather seats, and sulked all the way home.

My Sunburn Hates You

I was sprawled on the sofa, clad only in a pair of old-man boxers and a loose-fitting undershirt, when Jesse came home from the Sip-n-Stop. He'd pulled another ten-hour shift, and he was tired. Not too tired, though, to quip, "Shit, Sea—did your sunscreen, like, have a negative SPF?"

"Not funny," I moaned.

Critter came back from the kitchen bearing a Super Slushee cup of ice water. He sat on the edge of the couch and bent the big plastic fun straw so that I could sip the frosty goodness from a reclining position. Even my lips had burned to a blister, and little bits of whitish skin were starting to crack and flake.

"So I take it your little con worked?" Jess said, ripping off his Sip-n-Stop vest and basket-tossing it into a heap of dirty laundry in the middle of the room. "How was it?"

"Fine, until Miss Thang here decided to Kentucky fry her pale self."

I mustered up enough energy to punch Critter on his left shoulder blade. "Your fault," I muttered.

Multiple lines of sweat were dripping down Jesse's flushed face. "Goddamn, it's hot in here!" he said. He unbuttoned his white shirt and collapsed into the green velvet easy chair that lay perpendicular to my couch. Then he had the nerve to co-opt my small oscillating fan—the only source of cool air I had on my skin, which had become so hot to the touch I felt like I was going to spontaneously combust.

"Hey," I protested weakly. "I'm *hurt*, remember?"

"Did either one of you brainiacs think to call Mom?" Jesse said. "Hospital must have some magic potion that'd take the sting out."

Critter and I exchanged looks, because neither of us *had* called Nurse Layla. "I'm on it," Critter said, springing into action.

Jesse relinquished the fan and hopped upstairs for a quick shower. I closed my eyes, trying to remember what it was like to move my arm without sending searing pain up the length of it.

Critter thrust the phone in my face. "She wants to talk to you."

"Hey, sugar bear," Layla cooed through the phone. "Where's it hurt?"

"All over."

"You hot or cold?"

"Hot," I said. "Very hot."

"So no fever yet, that's good. Okay, Missy. Tell the boys to get you three aspirin, and flush them down with a whole lot of liquids. Water, not soda. I'll bring you some ointment on my dinner break, okay? Around seven or so. Until then, see if you can sleep it off."

"Will do," I murmured. "Love you."

"Love you too, hon."

Critter stood over me, looking a little anxious. "What'd she say?"

"Aspirin. Three. Why do you have that look on your face?"

"Mom sounded worried," he said. "You okay?"

I nodded. "I'll live."

He leaned down and placed a light kiss on the top of my head, but even my scalp was all burned up.

"Ow," I said.

"Oops, sorry. Let me get your meds."

I tried to sleep but couldn't, and by the time Layla bustled in, my inner heat had indeed turned to chills. She tossed me a thin box of ointment samples and commanded Jess to bring her a thermometer. I had a fever of about 102, and this made Layla frown. "I have to get back," she said. "But you boys keep an eye on her. I want hourly updates on her temp. If it hits one oh four, bring her in. And make sure she eats something, okay?" To me, she said, "Hold on there, sweetness. It'll be a rough night."

Jesse scurried into the kitchen to fix dinner; Critter's duty was to rip open the little foil packets so I could baste my body in some sort of sticky burn ointment. It took forever because the contents of each packet covered only about a square inch of skin. And it was awkward, rubbing that stuff on myself when I couldn't stop thinking about Sarah and her suntan lotion, and what had happened with Critter in the pool. Plus, it hard-core *stung*. I kept whimpering in pain, and each time, it made Critter look more miserable, which I had to admit was deeply satisfying.

"This," I said, "should teach you it doesn't pay to drool over Penn Acres princesses, no matter how manicured they are."

"I wasn't drooling," he protested. "Besides, you were the one who wanted me to mack on her in the first place."

"Whatever."

"Okay, okay," he said. "You gonna hate me forever?"

"I don't hate you," I said. "My sunburn hates you."

Critter grinned. "So what would it take for me and the burn to reconcile, hmm?"

"Ice cream."

He nodded gravely. "Yes, I can see how that might help. Let me finish painting you with the goop and then I'll pop out for some. Agreed?"

"Agreed."

Little. Pink. Good.

My fever broke early the next morning, not that I felt any different. I spent the night on the couch, soaked in sweat. My skin, which Critter and I had recoated with the ointment just before bed, kept sticking to the sheets we'd draped over the cushions. I couldn't sleep—couldn't even find a pain-free position to curl my body into during this state of hyper-awakeness. Late-night infomercials and the pint of Ben & Jerry's kept me semi-sane, even though Critter'd bought Phish Food (*his* favorite flavor), instead of the Cherry Garcia I'd asked for.

Layla stumbled in at six a.m., looking rougher than I felt. "You're up early," she said, kicking off her regulation rubber-soled shoes.

"More like late," I told her. "I hurt too much to sleep."

She frowned. "When's the last time you checked your temp?"

"Few minutes ago. It's back to normal."

With a suspicious "hrm," Layla scooped up the digital thermometer from the trunk we used as a coffee table, stuck it inside one of those plastic sleeves that protects the tip from people's germs, and said, "Open."

I didn't see the point, but it never does much good to argue with the Nurse. The edges of the plastic sleeve tickled my tongue and annoyed the piss out of me, but I waited the requisite minute. When the digi-beep went off, Layla removed the thermometer from my mouth and read the number—ninety-nine degrees. "Better," she said, "but not quite back to normal."

Fighting the urge to roll my eyes, I asked her if there

was something I could take that would kill the pain long enough for me to visit dreamland for a spell. I was really asking her if she'd give me a couple of her special pink pills, the ones she was pretty much forced to take when her anxiety was bad and insomnia set in. But the thing about Layla was this: even though she was a nurse, she was all about the New Age healing crap. With the exception of aspirin, she rarely allowed meds—even over-the-counter ones—into the house. One time she caught me with a pack of Midol and I had to sit through a thirty-minute lecture on how if I only took my vitamin B complex regularly, I wouldn't have cramps to begin with.

I must've looked really pathetic, because Layla simply reached into the white canvas tote that doubled as her purse and fished out a couple of her pinks. "My burnt bod and I thank you," I said, and threw the pills down my throat.

"I don't know how you do that without liquid."

"It's a gift."

"It's something," she said, chuckling. She reached behind her head and unclenched the plastic clip that kept her long hair up while she was at work. Layla's hair was the ashy-black color of cooled lava, and it slid all the way down to the middle of her rib cage. It was thick, too, and although she weighed at most about 110, I'd say at least 20 pounds of that was hair.

"Good night, my love," Layla cooed sleepily, and then planted a soft kiss on my tender forehead. "I'm back on at four, and I am exhausted."

"Me too."

The stairs creaked under Layla's feet, but the sound was distant, like I was hearing it through a glass. Suddenly my head felt like it was filled with jelly, and my eyelids closed like they had a mind of their own.

Let There Be Air

I slept hard and long. Next thing I knew, it was already dark again, and I was scooped up into Critter's arms.

"What're you doing?" I mumbled, my tongue thick and not exactly moving the way I wanted it to.

"Go back to sleep," I heard Jesse say from behind.

"Critter, put me down."

"No way," he replied. "I'm under strict orders."

We bounced up the steps, each bounce making more of my skin scream in pain. Critter kicked open the door to my bedroom and we moved inside.

Something was wrong.

"Cold?" I said.

"Cold," Jesse said.

The boys lay me down gently on the bed. It was too dark and I was too muddled to understand what was going on, but in a few seconds I registered the sound of a cranky rumble that could mean only one thing: air-conditioning.

Critter flicked on the light. Once my eyes adjusted, I saw it perched in the peeling wood pane of the window. It was bigger than our television and it shook so hard it made the glass rattle. But I didn't care about the awful sound. All I could focus on was the delicious arctic wave rippling across my tender skin.

"You like?" Jesse asked, with a big grin.

"I don't get it," I said. "How?"

"Jess took pity on you," Critter explained. "Bought it off that crazy lady at the Farmer's Market, the one who's always got like a hundred View-Masters on her table."

"We carried it home on the bus," Jesse added. If he'd been a cartoon character, his chest would've puffed out about a foot.

"You guys . . . you didn't have to do this."

"Of course not," Jesse said. "But Sea, you were

moaning something awful. We tried putting all the fans in front of you but you wouldn't stop. And the sweat! Man, it was starting to *stink*."

"Lovely."

"Hey, now," Critter said. "It wasn't your fault. It's the burn."

"Besides," Jesse added, "I sleep here, too. So it's not like the AC was entirely for your benefit."

"Speaking of," Critter cut in, "mind if I bunk on your floor? Just until this heat wave breaks."

"No way," I said. "You snore too loud."

"Yeah," Jesse said. "That's why I moved into her room in the first place, remember?"

"You guys suck." Critter lifted his chin like he was offended.

Ignoring him, I asked Jesse for the time. It was almost ten, and I hadn't eaten in what felt like a million years. "Hungry," I said. "Somebody feed me."

But the cold air felt so good, none of us wanted to leave the room. Critter got the idea that we should pool our spare dollars and call for pizza, because then only one of us would have to go back into the steamy parts of the house, and only for as long as it took to pay the delivery man. Except the phone was downstairs, so after a quick round of rock-paper-scissors, it was decided that Jesse would go get it and plug it into the jack in our room. Critter came in dead last, so it would be his job to pay the pizza guy upon arrival. They made me play, too, but God must've taken pity on me, because all I had to do was get waited on.

That's how we started moving everything into the twelve-by-twelve-foot room that Jesse and me shared. First the phone, then the big TV, and finally, the VCR and the stereo. We stayed in there as long as we could, except for taking bathroom breaks, grabbing more food and cold beverage from the kitchen, and in Jesse's case, going to work. It was like some kind of bizarre-o summer camp, only with electricity and better snacks.

This lasted a few days before Layla decided it was unhealthy for the three of us to be spending so much time in one little bedroom. She'd been weird about the living quarters since the winter before, when Jesse decided he should move into my space. Layla was totally against it, even though Critter's buzz saw snoring was keeping Jess up all night. Layla said if it was that bad, I should bunk with her, and Jess could have his own room. When that didn't work—Layla's highly irregular sleep schedule kept me from getting any real shut-eye—we went back to the original plan and Layla learned to deal. But she really put her foot down on this latest brainstorm. Our air-conditioned bliss ended with her ordering the boys to relocate the unit to the living room, along with the rest of our camp toys.

"This sucks," Critter said, wiping a band of sweat from his forehead. The two of us were on the couch, watching the copy of *Mallrats* that Shelli had stolen for Critter from the Movie King. Even with the air conditioner, the living room was muggy, because downstairs you couldn't really harness the cold.

"Agreed."

Critter cleared his throat. "What do you say we hit the pool again tomorrow?"

"Why?"

"For . . . you know, swimming. Tanning. Or in your case, *blistering.*"

I sat up. "For peeping Penn Acres princesses, is more like it."

"Oh, will you stop?" Critter slid off the couch onto the floor. "She wasn't all *that* cute. And she has a boyfriend, you know."

"Never stopped you before."

"You're the one who loves to swim," he said. "But whatever."

I crossed my arms over my chest. "Are you forgetting that I'm still pretty sizzled?"

"Not so much anymore," he said. "Just a little. And have you ever heard of a nifty thing called sunscreen?"

I sighed. "Fine. I'll go. But only if you can get Layla to loan you the car. I'm not taking three buses just so you can drool all over Miss Thang."

"Done," he said. "Just so you know, though . . . I don't give a smack about Sarah."

And in that one simple sentence, I knew. He used her actual name. Didn't even refer to her as "that Sarah chick" or some other variation, as was his style. No, she was simply "Sarah," and he simply had to see her again.

critter

Rock My Plimsoul

She was like a great song you hear on the radio but you don't know what it's called so you're not sure when—or if—you'll ever hear it again. A full week had crawled by and I couldn't shake her from my brain. Twice I'd gone to the Movie King for videos, and both times Shelli had made it clear she was available and I had actually *declined*. Told her I had strep throat. Told her it might be a while before I'd be clear to engage in that kind of activity again.

See, I didn't want Shelli; I wanted *her*. Sarah. And it wasn't just because she was hott-with-two-*t*'s. She had the kind of eyes that asked questions instead of passing judgments. I liked that. There was this other thing, too. Right before the Sea Monster had woken up from her sun scorcher of a nap, Sarah had been telling me about this song—a cover of Genesis' "Follow You, Follow Me" by Red House Painters—and she'd said, "It's so haunting and beautiful. . . . I just want to *live* in that song, you know?"

I told her she spoke my language, and she laughed. But I'd meant it. I had a feeling that this girl "got" me. Like she could see under my skin, find the place I kept hidden from almost everyone else, except maybe Seattle.

I had to see her again. *Had to*. Even if it meant bringing Sea along. What choice did I have? We did everything together. If I tried to sneak off, she'd get all suspicious and want to know *who* and *why* and *what*. Sea would do what she always did: point out exactly why I was attracted to this particular girl, why she was the worst possible choice I could make, and why the relationship (if it ever got to that stage) was doomed to fail in *x* number of months.

The worst part? Sea was usually right.

This time, I wanted to prove her *wrong*.

43

Let the Day Begin

I'd set my alarm for nine but woke up way before the buzzer went off. Totally unlike me, but so were the twitchy spasms in my suddenly nervous stomach. To ease them I sang my personal anthem—"Do Ya Think I'm Sexy?"—in the shower four full times before the water ran cold. It pumped me up, made me feel electric, like the spirit of Rod was running through my veins. It was working, too, until I realized that I was out of deodorant, and instead of grabbing Jesse's, I accidentally applied Seattle's, which smelled like baby powder. *Goodbye sexy!*

We set out just after eleven. I'd wanted to leave earlier, obviously, but Sea was dragging her ass. She said it was because she wasn't used to getting up before noon, but I think it was her way of trying to piss me off.

It worked.

"Why are you in such a rush?" she grumbled. "It's not like the pool's going anywhere." I told her I wanted to catch the prime tanning hours and she snorted. "I had sun poisoning, remember?"

"Yeah, but you're better now," I said. "And you can

butter yourself with sunscreen every fifteen minutes, okay? Let's just *go*."

After twenty minutes and a side trip to Dunkin' Donuts for coffee, we were on our way. The cracked leather seats in Layla's Cougar burned through my cargo pants and into my legs. The car was such a piece of shit, but Layla didn't believe in owning one you couldn't pay for outright. She made an art of driving junk cars into the ground. This one, though, was especially bad. Because it was in desperate need of a new muffler, it roared down the highway. Plus, both the AC and the radio were busted. And the bastard was so old, it actually had an eight-track tape player built into the dash, which meant if we wanted any music, we had to listen to Layla's vintage collection of Southern-fried rock.

"Think she'll like your ride?" Seattle said. "Or is the princess expecting you to roll up on a great white steed?"

"You better cut that out," I said.

"Why?" she asked snottily. "You afraid I'll embarrass you in front of your new girlfriend?"

I didn't answer; I just turned up the volume on some Steely Dan song I wasn't particularly fond of.

"C'mon, Romeo. Why's it so hard for you to admit you want to get in this girl's pants?"

"Because I don't," I said, feeling my jaw tighten.

"You're a liar."

"Why would I lie?"

"I heard you," she said flatly. "This morning. Your concert in the shower? I heard you."

Busted. I felt the corner of my left eye starting to twitch and I saw the smirk forming on Sea's face. So I shook my head and said, "Quit being stupid."

We didn't talk the rest of the way there.

Dynamite

The place was hopping. Two fat old men were sprawled out on lawn chairs, smoking stogies, their greased-up skin shining like freshly glazed Krispy Kreme donuts. Next to them lay a leathered forty-something chick with champagne-frosted hair, who, between puffs of her cigarette, erupted in this nasty, phlegmy cough. In the shallow end, there were three Golden Girls wearing loud floral-print suits, decked in full-on makeup and jewelry, their mouths moving like the moto-gossips I knew they had to be.

But where was my girl? The door to the pool supply closet was open, so I guessed she was poking around in there. I wanted to wait by the gate until she came out and I could catch her attention, but Sea wanted to turn around and go right home.

"This is stupid," she muttered. "She's not gonna let us in with all these people."

"You don't know that."

"Even if she did," Sea continued, "what kind of fun could we have, surrounded by the Geriatric League?"

Just then, Sarah emerged from the closet, her skin still radiating that soft golden glow. She was wearing a two-piece bathing suit this time, and the tank top was cropped a few inches above her belly button, showing off a stomach so tight that it would make even Halle Berry jealous. She'd pulled all of her hair into a messy bun, and there was a daisy stuck behind her right ear. It was more than sexy.

Sarah saw us and girly-jogged over to the gate. "Hi, guys!" she said, tucking a stray wisp of hair behind the unflowered ear. "I was wondering if I was ever going to see you again."

"We can't stay long," Sea informed her. "My skin is still recovering."

Sarah frowned. "What happened?"

"Oh, it was nothing," I said. "Just a little burn and a whole lotta complaining." Sea shot me a death glance but I ignored it and asked Sarah if we could come in. She looked around for a second, then grinned and said, "Screw it." I unlatched the gate and followed Sarah to her red canvas chair. There was an empty lounger a few feet away and I dragged it over to her spot and back-flopped onto it, which made Sarah laugh—exactly the reaction I was going for.

"Thank God you showed up today," Sarah said in a low voice. "The old biddies have been cranky since we opened. I needed some distraction."

I smacked a quick drumbeat on my belly and said, "I do what I can."

She grinned. "You do plenty."

It was like a well-scripted episode of one of those teen dramas on the WB, only it didn't star some thirty-year-old blonde playing a character half his age. It starred *me*.

Me and Sarah and a premenstrual Sea Monster determined to ruin my show, that is.

Seattle stormed over to where we were sitting and dropped her olive drab messenger bag at my feet. She was clawing at the contents like she was a rat and there was cheese hiding at the bottom, and I watched her for a few seconds before losing interest and turning back to Sarah. I was about to tell Sarah that I wanted to do a mix trade—a collection of underappreciated Rod Stewart gems in exchange for a grab bag of songs she wanted to "live in"—when Sea grunted loudly and dumped whatever was in her bag all over the hot concrete. Then she stamped her foot and barked, "Where did you put the sunscreen?"

"Excuse me," I said. "I believe I was having a conversation?"

"Listen, jackass," she spat. "The stupid sunscreen? It's not here."

I shrugged. "Maybe it's in the car."

"Well, can you go look for it?"

What was her deal? I wasn't about to let her embarrass me like that. So I said, "You got legs," and tossed her the keys.

As Sea stormed off, Sarah pretended to be interested in the Golden Girls, still yakking it up in the shallow end. This girl had *class*. "My sister," I said, shaking my head. "She's got more issues than a magazine rack."

"Don't we all."

Sarah reached into her knapsack, retrieved *her* bottle of Coppertone sunscreen, and started applying a thin layer to her face. For a second I wondered why she hadn't offered it to Sea, but then I got sidetracked by the way her skin was glistening in the light. "So how's Boyfriend doing?" I asked.

She locked the cap back into place. "Why are you so interested in Duncan?"

"I'm not," I said. "But I hear he's seeing this really fantastic girl, so . . ." I let my voice trail off meaningfully, but was confused when Sarah's smile twisted into an angry knot.

"Who?" she demanded. "What have you heard?"

"No, no," I said. "I meant *you*."

"Oh."

I knew if I didn't say something funny, the awkward tension would suffocate whatever kind of spark there was between us. "Damn," I said. "You sure know how to kill a guy's mojo."

"Sorry," Sarah said. "I didn't mean to snap." She lightly poked a pointer finger into my upper arm. "So you were flirting with me, huh?"

"Couldn't help it," I said, returning the friendly poke. "I have this condition that makes it impossible *not* to flirt with pretty girls."

"You're not so bad yourself," she said. "It's a shame I'm already spoken for."

Was that a warning? Or was it more like calculated encouragement? It didn't matter—I was more than eager to accept the challenge.

I ran the back of my finger across the arm of her chair, pretending I was caressing her thigh and not a piece of weather-beaten wood. "So when are we going to hang out?"

"We're hanging out now, aren't we?"

"I meant for real."

"What's that supposed to mean?"

I scratched at my chin. "You know," I said. "Going to the movies, maybe grabbing a bite to eat. The usual."

"Ah," she said, nodding. "You want to take me on a date."

I played innocent. "How could I take you on a date when you already have a boyfriend? Even if he is a thousand miles away."

"Try five hundred," she said. "But he's coming home for a visit real soon."

"Is that a no?"

She didn't answer me, not with words. Instead she leaned back in her chair, pulled a pair of silver shades over those big eyes, and smiled.

seattle

Grand Theft Auto

After a detailed search of the Cougar, during which no bottle of sunscreen surfaced, I stormed back to the pool area. Critter was still sprawled out on the lawn chair, maybe four inches from Sarah's canvas perch. He was saying something that made her touch that stupid flower in her hair and laugh, a light tinkling sound that reminded me of spaghetti-thin wind chimes. *Puke.* I threw the keys as hard as I could at Critter's bare stomach.

He shot up. "What the hell?"

"It's not there," I said.

"What's not there?"

"Are you kidding me? *The sunscreen!*"

"So what do you want me to do about it?"

"I want you to take me home," I said through semi-gritted teeth. "Now."

"Don't be silly," Sarah said. She dug into her yuppie bag and pulled out a sleek bottle. "Here, you can have some of mine."

"Yeah," Critter said. "Use some of hers."

I wasn't a crier. Never had been, not even when I was little. But at that moment, I wanted to cry. I wanted to throw myself down and beat my fists against the concrete and cry myself silly.

"Are you just going to stand there?" Critter said, staring at me with eyes shielded by one hand.

"No," I said, spying the car keys. "I'm going to *leave.*"

Before Critter could register what I'd said, I lunged down and grabbed the keys, turned on my heel, and walked away.

"Are you forgetting you don't have a license?" Critter yelled after me.

I flipped him the bird and kept on walking.

Benedict Critter

I spent the bulk of the afternoon curled up in my stuffy bedroom, crying so hard I couldn't breathe. How could Critter sell me out like that? So quickly and cleanly, like we didn't have eight years of history. Like we weren't partners in crime. He and Jesse shared blood, but me and Critter—I thought we had a bond even Jess couldn't penetrate.

We became best friends the first time our parents made us all go out together. My father had been dating Layla for a few months, and I'd been spending mad amounts of time with Colleen, this babysitter who ate all the good food (read: Tastykakes, Doritos, and Turkey Hill ice cream) in our apartment when she wasn't busy watching MTV or talking on the phone. I was seven, and far as I knew, my father hadn't really dated anyone since my biological mother's death (i.e., the Day I Was Born). Meeting Layla and her sons for the first time was new territory.

I still looked like a girl back then, my hair more like gold than like the colorless mass it turned when I hit puberty. Dad even paid Colleen extra to get me ready for the big night. She talked me into wearing the one dress I owned, a denim pinafore thing that went over a pink T-shirt, and she French-braided my hair, tying a little pink ribbon into a bow on the end of its tail.

We drove to Pappy's Pizzeria, my favorite. You could actually watch the guys make your pizza, and if you were extra-special nice, sometimes they'd toss you a piece of pepperoni through the opening between the kitchen and the bench you'd kneel on to watch. When we got there, Critter and Jesse were already on the watching bench, though Jesse was focused on his Game Boy. Standing beside them was Layla, who seemed to me like someone out of a fairy tale, with her long black hair swooping over one shoulder and down to her belly button. She hugged me by way of an introduction, and she smelled like peaches. I couldn't speak, afraid that I'd say the wrong thing and make her go away.

She introduced me to her boys—first Jesse, who lifted his head for a millisecond before plunging back into his game, and then Critter, whose first words to me were "Bet you can't catch a mushroom in your mouth."

"Sure I can," I said.

"Prove it."

I climbed onto the bench as Critter yelled, "Hey, pizza guy! Toss her a mushroom! A big wet one!"

Apparently this was a game they'd been playing—and losing—for a while, because the guy closest to us grinned, scooped up a mushroom with a spoon, and flicked it toward my head. I opened my mouth so wide it sailed in all the way to the back of my throat, and I accidentally swallowed it upon contact.

"Whoa," Critter said in awe. "You didn't even chew."

When we were getting seated, Critter insisted I sit between him and Jesse, so they could "share" me. Critter and I split a large birch beer, two straws in one giant red plastic glass, and Critter traded me his sausage chunks for my leftover crust.

Six weeks later, my dad and I moved out of our tiny apartment and into Layla's town house in New Castle. That first house—the one we lost when dear old Dad took off that final time, taking with him what little of Layla's savings he hadn't already drained—was like a mansion to me, with three full bedrooms, two bathrooms, and a finished basement that served as our playroom. Layla took me to Home Depot, and together we picked out a paint the color of new grass. It clashed horribly with the burnt-orange shag carpeting that was already in place, but I didn't mind. My new room had three windows, each covered in curtains Layla had sewn from a cheap purple velveteen fabric I'd also picked out myself. This, I decided, was what home was supposed to be like.

And for the next year and a half, I felt like I had one of those happy families that only exist on TV. But when Dad got laid off by GM, Layla picked up more shifts at the hospital to make up for his lost wages, and the fighting began. Big, loud, violent fights that made me and Critter and Jesse huddle up together on the bottom bunk in the room they shared. For the last six months that we were still a quote unquote family, my father disappeared four or five times for anywhere from three days to a week, without giving any notice or even an explanation when he got back. At least not to me.

Then he was just . . . gone. I spent the first month or so worrying—worrying that he wouldn't come back, worrying that he would. By the middle of the second month, it became pretty clear that if he wasn't gone for good, it would certainly be for a while.

Every so often I wondered how things would've

gone if Dad hadn't hooked up with a woman as won-derful as Layla. I couldn't imagine there were many single mothers out there who'd voluntarily take care of someone else's kid, especially if the kid's father had been the second guy to pretty much derail her entire life. But Layla had never debated my staying—lucky for me, because she was the only mother I'd ever known.

Family, it turned out, was something you really could choose for yourself.

•

It was almost six when I heard the screen door slam. I blew my nose into an already snotted-up paper towel and wiped my eyes with the back of my hand. The bedroom door swung open; I was surprised to see Jesse standing there.

"Hey," he said, doing a back flop onto his bed. "How was the pool?"

"Don't know," I said. "Didn't stay."

"Oh?"

"Long story."

Jesse turned onto his side, so that he was facing me. "So where's Critter?"

"I left him there."

"At the pool?"

I nodded.

"Didn't you guys take the car?"

I nodded again.

Jesse bolted upright. "You drove? What the hell were you thinking?"

"You don't understand," I said. "He was being . . . I don't know. *Mean.*"

"Oh, okay," he said, all sarcastic. "Yeah, I'm sure the cops would've accepted that instead of a driver's license. 'Sorry, officer, but my shit-head brother wasn't being very nice, so you see I simply *had* to take the car.'"

I didn't say anything, because it wouldn't have done any good. Once Jess got rolling with his dad routine, there was no stopping him.

"And what if you'd gotten into an accident, huh? You think Layla needs to get *that* call? Or worse, what if you'd just ended up in her ER? And forget about how much it would've cost to fix the goddamned car."

"Will you shut up?" I yelled. "Nothing happened."

Jesse shook his head in that disappointed-parent sort of way. "You're so stupid sometimes," he said. "One of these days you're gonna get your ass in some serious trouble."

I didn't feel like being lectured, so I stomped out of the room, down the stairs, and smack into Critter.

"Great," I said. "You wanna yell at me, too?"

"Dude, what's gotten into you?" he replied. "You're acting like a psycho."

"That's it?" I shrilled. "That's all you can say?"

He pressed his hand against my forehead. "Did your fever come back? Seriously, Sea, something is so not right."

I howled in frustration. Literally howled, a million decibels, square in Critter's face. Then I kneed him in the balls, grabbed my skateboard, and stormed right out the front door.

These Are the People in My Neighborhood

One problem with being best friends with your two faux brothers was that when you were pissed at both of them, there was no one you could vent to about it. Sometimes we hung out with other people, but the truth was we hated most of them. The only company we really enjoyed was each other's.

I threw my board onto the driveway and pushed off, coasting on the incline and popping from the curb onto flat ground. Instant exhilaration. I loved the sound my chewed-up wheels made as they spun across the asphalt.

Where to go? That was the question. Since I didn't have money, I couldn't bus down to the skate park. And it was too hot to haul tail down to Community Plaza, especially since the shopping center didn't even have any good ramps. There was always the generic, cheesy-ass playground toward the back end of our neighborhood. Its main feature was a cherry red metal merry-go-round that required the man power of at least two kids to get it moving at anything over a sluggish pace. Other than that, all the park had to offer were a semi-functional swing set and a teeter that didn't totter. Well, those and the fact that it was usually pretty quiet during the day. It wasn't until well after dark that the stoners co-opted the park for themselves.

The sun had almost set, but the temperature hadn't dropped much, and I was steaming by the time I got there. The wet air, thick like milk, made everything feel damp and moldy. I wanted to peel my skin off; that's how gross it was.

The merry-go-round came into view, and the fire inside me flared when I saw the neighborhood asshole, Russ Louten, sprawled on one of the sections. Russ was Critter's age, but a sophomore like me, and mostly I tried to avoid him and his super-baked crowd. Sitting in an adjoining section was some really tall guy I didn't recognize. I thought about turning back, but ignoring Russ Louten seemed infinitely more doable than dealing with the crap I'd left at home.

"Hey there, pretty lady," Russ called out. He was leaning back against the core of the merry-go-round, his legs spread as wide as possible, his left hand lazily scratching his stomach. I acted like I hadn't heard him and stamped over to the swing set.

Russ turned toward his friend and whispered something. He started cackling, but the tall guy nodded solemnly. Then Russ shouted, "What, you too good to talk to me now?"

"When did I ever talk to you, Russ?" I shot back. I leaned my board up against a pole and plopped heavily into the one working swing, smug and superior, then *wham!* The seat snapped off its hinge, dumping my ass onto the dirt. *Hard.*

"Ooh, shit!" Russ screeched. "Yo, Aiken, you been packing on the pounds?" Ignoring his cackle, I struggled to stand, leaving my last bit of dignity in a cloud of dust. As I brushed the filth off my baggy black pants, I heard the tall guy call out, "You okay there?"

"Yeah," I said. "Just fine."

"Come over here," Russ commanded. "I want to introduce you to someone."

The tall guy offered a stoic smile and wave. He was wearing a *Matrix*-style trench coat—even in this heat—and something about that made me want to know who he was. I tucked my board under one arm and sauntered over, trying to look as disinterested as possible.

"Seattle Aiken, as I live and breathe," Russ said, a slimy grin oozing across his ugly freckled face, "this is my cousin, Scooter. Scooter's visiting from your namesake, aren't you, Scooter?"

"*Scooter?*" I said. "You've got to be kidding me."

"Sadly, no," Scooter said. "But nobody calls me Scooter anymore. Just Scott."

"Huh."

Russ reached out for my board, but I jumped backward before he could touch it. He made a face and said, "Jesus, I wasn't going to take it." I mumbled an apology and he rolled his eyes. "All's I was going to say is that Scooter's into that skater crap, too."

"Yeah?" I said. "What kind of ride you got?"

"Darkstar deck," he said. "Thunder trucks. They've got *great* control."

"What kind of wheels?" I asked Scott.

"Spitfire Daggers."

"Nice."

A grin broke across his face. "I like to think so." He nodded toward my board. "What do you have there?"

"An old Kryptonics. It's pretty much lost its pop. Element put out this Fiberlight deck I've been eyeing, but I don't have the cash."

"You don't have to break the bank," Scott said. "Get a blank deck and build it yourself. If you run into the right deals, you could have a new complete for around sixty bucks."

"You build your own?"

"You know it."

"Sick," I said, impressed.

"I could help you," he offered. "Russ, your dad's got a drill, right?" Russ nodded, clearly bored by all the skate talk. To me Scott said, "I'm here for the summer. I can teach you how to build a board, deck up."

"That'd be awesome."

Scott flashed me another grin and looked away. He had this strong jawline, all angles. And his skin was so clear, the kind that usually belonged to airbrushed underwear models. When he turned back, I saw his eyes, large as quarters and steely blue. They were framed by the longest lashes I'd ever seen, on a girl or a boy.

"This place is tired," Russ said, hopping off the merry-go-round. "Let's bail."

Scott nodded, still solemn, still staring right at me. I let my eyes fall to his lips, a deep wine color and so so plump.

Russ jutted his chin at me. "You coming?"

"Yeah," Scott said, cocking his head. "You should come with us."

"Where to?"

Russ shrugged. "Does it matter?"

And then it hit me: "We should go to my place."

"My kind of girl," Russ purred, reaching down to muss my hair.

I swatted his hand away. "You wish."

Russ turned to Scott and stage-whispered, "I forgot. Seattle doesn't like boys. She's hard-core butch."

"I so am *not*."

"You got proof?"

I jammed my hands onto my hips. "What kind of proof do you need?"

He grabbed his crotch. "I got your proof right here."

Scott punched Russ in the arm. "Show some respect."

"Screw you, then," Russ shot back, scowling and rubbing his arm. "I'm out of here, man."

"I'll catch up with you later," Scott yelled to Russ.

I smiled. "Then I guess it's just you and me."

There's a Boy in My Bedroom

They'd locked me out. It took about six rings of the doorbell before Jesse let me in. I stormed by him, my board in one hand and Scott's hand in the other, dragging Scott through the house without bothering to introduce him. We went upstairs into my room, where I found Critter rooting through a stash of Jesse's magazines.

"Out," I said. He looked at me, eyes wide in surprise. "I said get out!"

The surprise turned to anger, and Critter sprung up and thundered out of the room, slamming the door behind him.

"Better," I said. I plopped onto my bed, kicked off my shoes. Scott towered over me. "Why don't you sit down?" He squatted on the floor. "I meant here," I said, patting the mattress beside me. With a shy smile, Scooter scooted up next to me.

"Hi," he said.

"Hi."

Now that I had him there, I wasn't sure what to do with him. After a short uncomfortable silence, I asked, "So how long have you been skating?"

"Almost six years," Scott replied. "Since I was twelve."

I grinned. "I got you beat."

"Really?"

"Yeah," I said. "I started when I was eight."

"Impressive."

I shrugged. "My brother—the one I just kicked out—Critter was the one who wanted to be a skater. He got a board for his tenth birthday—you know, like the kind you'd get at Toys "R" Us? Only he couldn't do more than glide a couple feet on asphalt before wiping out, so he gave it to me. I was popping ollies within a week."

"You're a natural."

I shrugged again. "I just like it, is all."

"So what else do you like?" he asked, nudging my shoulder with his. Was he coming on to me? Before I could figure it out, Scott bent over and picked up a book off the carpet. It was *Biology Made Simple*—the first of about a dozen texts Layla had brought home for me and Critter, to get us ready for summer school. As if we'd waste our time reading that crap.

"Give me that!" I snatched the book out of Scott's hands and threw it across the room, where it landed on Mount Saint Laundry—Jesse's nickname for the pile of clothes I let accumulate before actually washing any of them.

"You act like it's porn!" Scott said, laughing. "There's nothing wrong with being into science."

I could feel my face turning red. "It's not like that."

"So what is it like?"

"Look, I don't want to talk about biology, okay?"

What I really wanted was to be kissed. *Hard.*

"Do you wanna fool around or what?" I blurted out.

Scott laughed again. "Are you serious?"

Not exactly the response I had been hoping for. I folded my arms across my chest and said, "Why wouldn't I be?"

He shrugged. "I don't know."

"You don't have to worry," I said. "I'm not looking for a boyfriend or anything."

"So what *are* you looking for, then?"

I pulled him to me so suddenly and so fiercely that even I was surprised. He tasted like cherry cough drops, and man, could that cat *kiss*. He rolled me onto my back; I could feel his hard-on through both our pants. It made me even hotter, and I broke out in a sweat. My hands clawed at his lower back, pressing him into me.

We rolled over again, and then I was on top, my knees anchored on the sides of his waist. I shook out my dreads and looked down, surprised that Scott's face sported a super-serious look, like we were getting ready to take the SATs instead of maybe doing it. He fingered one of the ropy blue strands like it was alien hair.

Before I could overthink things, I grabbed the hem of my T-shirt and pulled it off over my head. Thankfully, I was wearing one of my "good" bras—a satiny turquoise underwire that pushed my droopy overgrown boobs into something vaguely resembling hot-girl cleavage. Scott's face softened, and a smile appeared on his lips.

"Oh," he whispered.

I thought it was a good "oh," but I must've misread the situation, because when I reached behind me and started to undo the clasp, Scott said, "Wait a second."

"What?"

He propped himself up on his elbows. "Maybe we should slow down a bit."

Translation: *I don't want to see you naked.*

I climbed off him almost as quickly as I'd climbed on, heat seeping into my cheeks. Of course the first time I tried to play the femme fatale, I'd get rejected. I haphazardly fished around for the T-shirt I'd just taken off.

"You're angry," Scott said.

I didn't answer.

"Listen," he began. "You're cute as hell, but honestly? I try not to sleep with a girl before I've known her . . . oh, I don't know. At *least* an hour." He let out a little laugh, as if to let me know that the last bit had been a joke, but it sounded totally forced.

Finally, I found the T-shirt and in my haste managed to put it on both backwards and inside out. I started to pull it off again to fix it, but before I could, the bedroom door swung open and I froze.

Critter.

"Don't you knock?" I seethed, pulling the T-shirt back down.

"What did you do with the car keys?" he asked coldly. "It's time for me to pick up Layla. Unless, of course, *you'd* rather do the honors."

"Screw you."

Scott stood up and said, "I guess I should be going."

"Wait!" I said. "Just give me a sec."

He shook his head. "I'll see you around, okay?" He brushed past Critter with a customary nod and left without so much as a kiss goodbye.

"Could you speed it up?" Critter asked. "You know how Layla hates to be kept waiting."

"You're unbelievable." I picked through Mount Saint Laundry, looking for the misplaced keys. "What, are you the only one in this house allowed to get your jollies?"

"Forgive me for interrupting this truly meaningful occasion," he spat. "I'm sure Layla would love to know I'm late because her daughter was too busy doing some stranger to find the car keys she stole."

"I wasn't 'doing' him," I said hotly.

"Whatever. Just get me the goddamned keys, okay?"

I dug around for a few minutes before locating

them inside a sneaker. Critter watched me the entire time, staring me down with his icy eyes. I threw the keys at him as hard as I could and yelled, "Now get out!"

He slammed the door behind him.

critter

I Don't Want to Talk About It

"Driving is an attitude."

That was the only helpful nugget of wisdom that Frank, my long-gone sorry excuse for an almost-stepfather, ever imparted to me. I was all of ten years old when he said it, but for some reason, it stuck. It was the first thing I said to myself whenever I slipped behind the wheel of a car. The words got especially loud on days like the one I'd just had. Days I got so mad I could punch a window, just to hear the crack of bone on glass.

It was almost nine and I was still a good fifteen minutes from the hospital. Mom was gonna be pissed. Then she'd ask me why I was late, and I sure as shit wasn't going to tell her about walking in on Sea and that dude. Or about how Sea had taken the car earlier. No need to get Mom all worked into a froth over nothing.

The sides of my head felt like they were being squeezed together. The pain was so intense I thought I might hurl, even though I hadn't eaten since breakfast. When I was just a kid I used to get these migraines, always on the left side of my head, that would get so bad I'd black out. They stopped right before I turned eleven—not so long after Frank ran off for good, the bastard.

I hadn't factored in the construction on I-95. Three lanes poured into one, inching along, fan-freaking-tastic. My knee jiggled under the wheel. I hated just sitting. Lately I needed movement, needed *go go go*. Maybe it was that girl. Sarah. She was hot enough to light anyone's engine.

It was 9:18 when I finally squealed into the parking

lot. Mom was standing outside, scowling. She'd barely opened the passenger-side door when I said, "Don't even start with me."

"And a lovely evening to you, too," she said. "Want to tell me why you're such a ray of sunshine?"

"Not especially."

"Okay, then."

We drove back onto 95, where traffic in the opposite direction was backed up 'cause the drivers were dumb enough to stare at the idiots who were backed up on the other side. I smacked the steering wheel. Mom looked at me. "I take it you didn't have a good time at the pool," she said.

"Pool was fine."

"Did you bring that SAT book I got you? How many practice tests have you taken so far?"

"All of them," I said, voice dripping sarcasm. "Got perfect scores. Harvard's gonna waive my application, that's how smart I am."

Mom sighed. I could tell she was annoyed with me, but I really didn't feel like talking about all of the bullshit. Instead, I said, "Are you hungry? I haven't eaten in, like, a zillion years."

"You guys didn't have dinner?"

"Not really."

"Not really or no?"

"No, okay? Everyone was in a pissy mood, so we all went our separate ways."

"Great," Mom said. "Good thing I left you guys that tuna casserole."

"You mean the one we ate three days ago?"

She sighed again. "Pull into the Mickey D's."

I got off at the next exit and slid the Cougar into the parking lot at McDonald's. "Let's skip the drive-through," I said. I wasn't all that psyched about getting back home.

"What about Jess and Sea?"

"We'll get theirs to go." Mom shrugged in agreement.

As I tore into my Double Quarter Pounder with extra extra cheese, Mom gave it another shot: "So are you going to tell me what this is all about?"

I dropped the burger back onto its paper wrapper. "Sea and I got into a fight. A kicking-me-where-it-counts kind of fight."

"Literally or metaphorically?"

I chuckled. "Literally, of course."

"Oh."

I pushed some fries around the mountain of shared

ketchup. Mom asked me if I wanted to talk about it and I said no. Then she got this sour look on her face, and I knew if I didn't say something to satisfy her curiosity, she'd keep poking at me. "It's nothing. Really," I said. "It'll all blow over in a day or two."

Her eyes narrowed. "You can't lie for shit, so don't bother trying."

The throbbing in my head got harder. Even chewing was starting to hurt. I sighed, wadded up the rest of my burger in its grease-stained wrapper, and said, "Let's get out of here."

Dishevelment Blues

Back at the Bat Ranch, Jess and the Sea Monster were making scrambled eggs and bacon, the smell of which filled the whole first floor. Guess they didn't need take-out after all. I was about to say something snarky when I heard Seattle's jelly-belly laugh float into the hallway. It made me feel both relieved and annoyed.

"I need a shower," Mom said, climbing the stairs. "Tell them I'll be down in a bit."

I headed into the kitchen and tossed the greasy paper sacks onto the countertop. "What's cooking?" I asked.

"What's it look like?" Jesse answered. "You want some?"

"Nah, I just ate. Brought you guys some, too."

"Awesome," Jesse said. "Looks like we got ourselves a two-course meal."

Seattle had gotten really quiet when I'd walked into the room. No jelly-belly laughs for my benefit, thank you very much. She was standing near the toaster, staring at it like the bread wouldn't toast if she didn't keep her eyes glued to it the entire time. I wanted to say something, but I wasn't sure what, so I said nothing. Instead I watched Jesse slide bacon from a skillet onto a paper-toweled plate. It looked so good, I couldn't help stealing a fresh strip. It burned my fingers, and I yelped in pain.

"That's why you're supposed to wait until it cools, dumb-ass," Jesse said. Just to piss him off, I picked up the strip I'd just dropped and shoved the entire length of it into my mouth. Jess shook his head in that disapproving way of his, and I rolled my eyes and asked him if he wanted to watch a movie.

He shook his head. "I've got some stuff to take care of after dinner."

"Stuff?"

"Yeah, stuff. Don't you?"

"What's that supposed to mean?"

"There's good TV on," Seattle cut in. "A *Simpsons* marathon on channel four."

"Whatever," I said.

I didn't feel much like hanging with Homer, so after downing four ibuprofen I took from Sea's and my secret stash, I went into the living room and popped in the mid-nineties classic *Clueless*. It was one of those movies crawling with cute girls—Alicia Silverstone, with the big doe eyes and that deliciously frowny mouth; Stacey Dash, she of the coffee-and-cream complexion and legs that refused to quit; and a pre-blond, pre-anorexic Brittany Murphy, shaking her juicy bubble to Coolio, of all people.

I must've passed out, because the next thing I knew, the credits were rolling and the house was dark. And quiet. No lights, no radio, no nothing. I checked the upstairs and saw Layla snoozing peacefully, but otherwise the place was empty. That pissed me off, because if anyone got left behind, it was usually Jesse. Now I was the cheese, and I didn't like it. Not one bit.

In my pocket was the slip of paper Sarah had given me earlier, after Seattle had taken off. I didn't need it anymore; I'd already committed the digits to memory. It was almost eleven-thirty, which was probably too late to call. Even if it wasn't, it wouldn't look good to call her so soon. Tomorrow, maybe. Or the day after that.

Thoroughly frustrated, I went back downstairs, flopped onto the couch, and fell into an angry sleep.

In a Broken Dream

I was on a boat. A big one, the kind Frank used to take us fishing on out in the Chesapeake. It was hot out, and I wasn't wearing a shirt, just a pair of jeans that had been cut at the knees. All I could see for miles and miles was water that was too blue to be real.

She was there. Sarah. Standing on the deck next to me, wearing a tiny bikini top and that crazy wrap skirt she'd had on the first time we met. Her hair was hanging past her shoulders and blowing around in the wind, like she was some kind of *Sports Illustrated* swimsuit model. And, oh—her feet. Bare and brown, with perfect little toes.

I couldn't stop staring at her feet.

Her hand reached out for the waistband of my jeans and tugged me forward. Her fingertips touched my naked stomach and I popped an instant chubby. She didn't say anything; she just leaned forward into my neck with a firm kiss. Her hair smelled like Coppertone, or maybe it was her shoulder.

The boat rocked a bit, making me stumble. I held on to her for balance. Her nipples were hard; I could feel them against my chest. She pulled me even closer. I untied the knot on her skirt and it flew away. I hooked my thumbs on the side strings of her bikini bottoms and pulled them down some. The tan line alone just about killed me.

The only thing left between us was my jeans, but I couldn't get them undone, like the button had been rusted shut. I pulled at it harder and harder, getting frantic, feeling like I was going to explode if I couldn't get inside of her *right that second*.

A throaty voice said, "Want some help with that?" But when I looked up, it was my honey Alicia Silverstone, with her doe eyes and frowny mouth.

Only, her hair was blue.

First Cut Is the Deepest

I woke up violent-style, coated with sweat. Seattle was sitting on the edge of the couch, her face scrunched up in concern. "You okay?" she asked. "You look kind of sick."

"I'm fine," I snapped. "Why are you watching me sleep?"

"I wasn't," she shot back. "I wanted to give you this." She handed me a damp paper cup from Rita's. It was filled with my favorite gelato: vanilla frozen custard swirled with root beer water ice.

"Thanks," I mumbled.

"It was supposed to be a peace offering, but whatever." She got up and made like she was going to leave.

"Don't go," I said. "I didn't mean to bark at you. You just scared me, is all."

Seattle sighed and tugged at one of her fading-blue dreadlocks. "I don't like it," she said.

"Don't like what?"

"Fighting," she said. "Duh."

"Oh."

I spooned some of the gelato into my mouth, and then, as a token of my appreciation, offered Sea her own spoonful. She shook her head. "Jess and I already had some."

"Of course."

The tension between us was thicker than my custard. And I was still messed up from my freaky dream, so I couldn't think of anything to say that might clear the air. I kept slurping down my gelato, even though the coldness was bringing on a fresh wave of headache.

Sea kept pulling on her dreadlocks. "I hate my hair," she said.

"Since when?"

"Since now. I feel like cutting it all off."

"Okay," I said. "Bring me the shaver and I'll do it for you."

She gave me a blank stare. "Do what? Make me bald?"

I shrugged. "Sure, whatever. Could be kind of cute."

"Bald," she said again, her voice flat.

"Yeah," I said. "Bald."

Now it was like some kind of challenge. When she wordlessly walked out of the room a minute later, I thought she'd backed down. Instead, she returned with a pair of scissors and the electric shaver in hand.

"So go ahead," she said, offering them up like some kind of sacrifice. "Do it."

Was she bluffing? I couldn't tell. I needed more time to chew this over, so I tipped my Rita's cup at her and said, "Can I finish, please?" She nodded, and I slowed my slurp pace. Seattle dropped to the floor, crossed her legs pretzel-style, and after resting her chin in her hands, fixed her eyes on me. Watching me eat with the same intensity she'd watched the toaster with earlier.

It was good, though; it gave me time to imagine what she'd look like without any hair. She had a round face—not fat, but soft and circlelike. A baby face. Big, big eyes, dark brown and set deeply. Cute nose—smallish, and round on the tip—and a plush mouth, small but full, like Angelina Jolie's if hers had been run through a Shrinky Dinks machine.

I guessed I had been staring at her too long, because she said, "Memorized me yet? Eat up, Sparky. You've got work to do."

Her calling me out like that made me feel itchy, so I pushed my plastic spoon aside and drank the melted remains of my gelato. "Okay," I said. "Hop to it, *Sparky.*"

I sat on the edge of the couch while Sea scooted between my legs. "Scalpel?" She handed me the scissors. "Are you sure about this?" I asked the back of her head. "It's not like that doll you used to have. I can't just crank your arm and make it go back."

"Do it."

Seattle and I had been cutting and dyeing each other's hair almost as long as we'd known each other, so it shouldn't have been a big deal. But it was. Snipping off that first faded-blue dread made me wince. I held the fat worm of hair in my palm. It felt wrong.

"Keep going," Sea said firmly.

I laid the blue lock, matted into its twisted shape, next to me on the couch cushion. The next five or so came off kind of quickly, and I dropped them on the floor next to Seattle's left knee. I half expected her to pick one up, but she didn't even look down, not once.

When all the dreads had been cut, there was maybe a half inch of scraggly white-blond hair tipped in blue left on her head. She looked like a chemo patient. I didn't know if I could finish the job.

"You wanna take a look?" I asked her. "It's pretty punk rock right now."

"No, you said bald."

"I know what I said. Doesn't mean you have to do it."

She lifted the shaver defiantly, like she was the Statue of Liberty and it was her torch. After thirty seconds of awfulness, I snatched it from her and flipped the On switch, hoping that the batteries were dead. They weren't.

"Go on," she urged. "Do it."

The itchiness returned; flash pops of my freaky dream kept exploding in my head. Blue hair, frowny mouth, Sarah's half-naked bod. I shook them off and, with one smooth motion, carved a road through what was left of Seattle's hair.

Five minutes later, she had nothing but fuzz coating her scalp. "There," I said. "Are you happy?"

She pulled herself up and went into the bathroom to check out my handiwork. I couldn't watch. I started to clean up the hair, but when a couple of minutes had passed and she hadn't returned, I had to go see if she was okay.

She'd left the door open and was standing in front

of the small circle mirror. Her hands were on the back of her head, rubbing it slowly, like she couldn't believe it was gone. I felt like such an asshole. How could I have made her bald? Why had I egged her into it? I was a shit, plain and simple.

Slowly, Seattle turned around. When she did, I was surprised to see how good she looked without any hair. A grin spread across her face. "I love it," she said. "Thank you." She threw her arms around my neck and kissed me on the cheek. That would've been fine, if I hadn't been quite so conscious of her double-D cleavage squeezed against my chest.

I was more than glad when she finally pulled away.

Dancin' Alone

My sister had breasts.

She'd always had them, I supposed. I just wasn't sure when they'd gotten quite so *big*. Seemed like only yesterday she was pancake flat. Then again, she usually wore really baggy shirts, and who knew what was hiding under them? The last time I'd seen her in anything remotely figure-forming was when she wore her bathing suit, but it was black and had a high neck and made her look more like a spinster than a girl with a great rack.

My sister was not supposed to have a great rack. At least, not one that I noticed.

Since the shower had always been my refuge, I decided to pop in and shake things off, so to speak. I started to do what I always did: turn the water on full blast, wait until it was good and steamy-hot, and then boil my skin, which I'd continue to do until the spray ran cold. This was my ritual. The first six minutes consisted of standing in front of the stream, doing nothing except taking in the heat, feeling it beat on my back. Then I'd smoosh a squirt of Pert Plus into my hair, and rinse. Soaping up my bod took all of two minutes, and then I'd spend the rest of the shower jerking off. I'd gotten the timing down so good that I usually managed to finish about fifteen seconds before the water turned to ice, the coldness a pleasant shock to my warm post-orgasmic state.

Tonight's shower, though, was proving difficult. I couldn't stop thinking about what it felt like, Sea's enormous boobs making direct contact with my chest. And of course this made me wonder what they looked like, which in turn made me feel like a nasty pervert. She was practically my *sister*. I finally understood what Shelli must've gone through the time she walked in on her mom fooling around with the plumber. It was like someone had stamped an image on your brain against your will, and there wasn't anything you could do to make it go away. I balled my hands into fists and pressed them into my eyes, trying to erase what I was seeing in my mind.

I could feel the stirrings of a hard-on and hoped it was an automatic response to this phase of the shower, and not some sign that I was morphing into a full-on perv. Just to be certain, I conjured up some surefire fantasy material. Sarah, naked, and begging for it. I closed my eyes tight, focusing on her pressed up against me in that boat from my dream, and reached down. But I'd barely found the rhythm when Seattle's newly bald head stuck itself on Sarah's shoulders.

I wanted my hand to stop but it wouldn't. A few tugs later and it was over, Sea's head still clouding up my mind. I felt so dirty that I soaped up all over again, even though the water had turned cold. *Serves me right,* I thought. *What kind of sicko shoots his load when his sister's on his mind?*

seattle

What Goes Up Must Come Down

The next morning I woke up around nine—early, at least for me. My body ached to skate. Screw the heat; I'd make myself immune. I put on some baggy pants and poked around Mount Saint Laundry for a semi-clean T-shirt. They all smelled like feet, so I grabbed one of Jesse's out of his dresser. We were about the same height, but he had smaller bones, and the front of his shirt stretched so tightly across my chest that the hem of it barely covered my belly button. This was not ideal—I was used to hiding my curves, not showing them off—but I had no time for vanity. I was itching to get on my board.

I thought I could get out the door without Critter noticing, but when I went into the kitchen to grab some breakfast, there he was, leaning on the counter, dunking a Pop-Tart into his usual mug of Coke.

"You're dressed," he said.

"I'm going skating."

"How are you even awake?"

I shrugged. "How are you?"

He crammed the last of the Pop-Tart into his mouth and swallowed. "You want me to go with you?"

"Nah," I said. "I kind of want to be alone."

It was rare that Critter and I did things on our own. But the day before had been so weird, what with him walking in on me and Scott. And since my morning agenda included finding Scott, I knew it wouldn't be appropriate to bring Big Brother along. So I tossed him a quick "later," and went on my way.

First I skated to the park where I had run into Scott and Russ, but it was empty. Of course. Why would anyone be up and out at this insanely early hour? So then I skated over to Russ's street. There was a metal bike rack on the end of it that no one ever used. It was a great surface for practicing lipslides—which also gave me a viable excuse for being near Russ's place to begin with.

Halfway there I realized I'd left my pads and helmet at home. It was pretty stupid to do lipslides on a high rail without any sort of protective gear, but going back to get it meant facing Critter again—not an option.

For a skater, confidence is key. The minute I started to doubt a landing, I fell. It was as simple as that. If I flew on autopilot, never questioning the position of my wheels, I almost never bailed.

I tried to keep this in mind as I ollied up the curb onto the sidewalk. The plan was to launch into the lip-slide on the first pass, but as I popped the next ollie, I got spooked and landed it without even attempting the rail. *Mistake No. 1.* On the second pass, my back foot slipped, so instead of smacking the tail of my board down into the ollie, I smacked my tailbone against the hard concrete. *Mistake No. 2.*

This was when I should've chucked it all and just gone home. But messing up the ollie—the basis for most skate tricks, so easy even six-year-olds can land them in their sleep—was a slap to my pride. Now I *had* to nail the lipslide.

I picked up speed, popped the perfect ollie, and turned my board so that when I landed on the metal rail, it was snug up against the inside of my rear trucks. The lipslide itself was flawless. And if it hadn't been for a stray cat crawling along the spot where I planned to land, everything would've been beautiful. But since killing said cat would be a bad thing, I kicked my board away midair, sending it off to a soft patch of grass and me to a particularly choppy piece of asphalt.

Mistake No. 3.

A string of particularly loud obscenities shot out of my mouth as the pain spread to every inch of my body. There were small pebbles embedded in several sections of skin, and blood trickled from my left ankle and elbow. The only saving grace was that no one was around to witness the carnage.

Wrong. Not ten seconds later a concerned-looking Scott came jogging across the parking lot, naked except for a pair of camo pants hacked off just below the knee. "Are you okay? Is anything broken? Can you move your arm? Your leg?"

I wanted to respond but couldn't make my mouth work. It was mostly from the shame of knowing he must've seen me wipe out, but the small chunk of glass sticking out of my bottom lip didn't help either.

"Jesus," Scott said. "You don't do anything halfway, do you?"

Before I could stop him, he helped me up off the ground, threw my right arm around his neck, and half carried me back to Russ's house.

Doctor Love

"Stop squirming."

Scott was pressing a cotton ball soaked in peroxide against the spot where he'd tweezed out the glass, and it burned like hell.

"I said stop squirming."

I pushed his arm away. "Get that thing off me."

"You want an infection?"

"I want a painkiller."

He laughed. "Quit your bitchin' and let me fix you up."

Despite my protests, I sort of liked the feel of Scott's fingertips on my face. Plus, he was still shirtless, so I was getting an up-close-and-personal view of the fine black hair skimming the nicely defined muscles of his chest. The only thing I didn't like about this scene was the locale (i.e., Casa de Louten). Thankfully, His Royal Russ-ness was still bunkered down from the night, so it was almost like Scott and I had the place to ourselves.

"It hurts," I moaned.

"Here," he said, offering me his other hand. "Squeeze it."

I squeezed as hard as I could—at first. But the more he talked, the more I loosened my grip. Eventually there was no squeezing involved, and we were simply holding hands.

"You know," he said, "you were looking pretty good out there. Got a lot of air between you and the ground."

"Thanks."

"You're right about that board, though. It's definitely seen better days."

"I know," I said. "But skating's an expensive hobby. And Layla—that's my mom—she says my grades aren't high enough for me to spend time working when I should be studying."

He cocked his head. "So pull up the grades. You have to work if you want to support your habit."

How many times had Jesse said the exact same

thing to me? And how many times had those words made me feel super defensive and more than a little pissed off? Now I just felt ashamed, like Scott thought I was some kind of stupid slacker girl.

He tossed the soiled cotton ball into the bathroom's wastebasket and let go of my hand. "Let me see that elbow."

I thrust it upward and said, "I'm not dumb, you know."

"No one said you were."

"I meant about the grades. School's stupid. I hate the people and I'm always bored."

Scott smiled patiently, somehow avoiding the look of condescension that usually went with that sort of smile. "You do what you have to do, right? I mean, don't you ever think about going to college?"

"Not really." My eyes narrowed into full-on squint position. "How old are you, anyway?"

"I'll be eighteen in September."

"And do *you* ever think about going to college?"

"Already been," he said. "Evergreen State. Just finished my first year."

"At seventeen?"

"I'm a nerd," he said, almost sheepishly. "My mom

had me in kindergarten when I was four, and I tested out of my senior year in high school."

"Oh."

The brainiac finished with my elbow and tapped on my banged-up knee. "Evergreen's a really progressive liberal arts school. Lots of hands-on stuff, less time spent talking theory. I almost never get bored."

I rolled my eyes. "Are you trying to recruit me?"

"Yes," he said. "That's exactly what I'm trying to do. I totally get off on converting people to the Cult of Formal Education." He punctuated the sentence by squeezing my non-hurt knee, so even though I wanted to be annoyed, all I could really do was smile.

He asked me if I'd had breakfast and I told him no. "Well, pretty girl, this is your special day. We've got a brand-new box of Lucky Charms sitting in the pantry."

Automatically I reached up to tug on a dreadlock, forgetting for a second that I no longer had any hair. Pretty girl? Not me.

"I cut my hair," I blurted out.

"Really? You did?" I was about two seconds from being crushed when a big grin spread across Scott's face. "I'm kidding. I think it's really cute."

"Cute?"

"Yeah, it makes your eyes stand out. You couldn't see how pretty they are behind all that blue hair."

There was that word again. *Pretty.* But I wasn't a pretty girl. At least, I'd never thought of myself as one.

My stomach did a flip-flop. *Danger, Will Robinson.* I had a feeling I shouldn't get too excited about a seventeen-year-old genius boy who went to college three thousand miles away, even if he could skate.

"You never mentioned why you're here for the summer," I said. "I can't imagine your cousin's charms are the draw."

He nodded. "I was waiting for you to ask that question."

"And?"

"Well . . . I was supposed to spend the summer in Austin, with my girlfriend."

Girlfriend?

"*Ex*-girlfriend," he corrected himself. "Her uncle's an indie filmmaker shooting his first full-length feature. We were going to work on the set, do some grunt work."

"So what happened?"

"I walked in on her having sex with my roommate."

"Oh." It took a minute for his words to sink in.

"*Oh,*" I said again. Genius Skater Boy was actually Genius Skater *Rebound* Boy.

"Look," Scott said, "there's nothing going on between Katja and me. I'm almost completely over it."

Katja. Now *that* was the name of a pretty girl. "If you're so over it," I said, "why did you have to come all the way to Delaware to heal your broken heart?"

"What was I supposed to do? Sit at home and mope? I'd already bought my plane ticket to Austin. I didn't want it to go to waste, so . . ."

I sat there, totally silent. Scott poured another dose of Lucky Charms into his bowl and crunched along, staring into space as I tried to sort things out. I wasn't the most experienced dater, but I had a feeling that Genius Skater Boy + recent ex-girlfriend + college three thousand miles away = disaster waiting to happen.

So we'd be friends. It wasn't like I had a ton of those, anyway.

Just then a beyond-bedheaded Russ wandered in, also naked save a pair of Incredible Hulk boxers. He took one look at me, rolled his eyes, and said, "What happened to your hair? Is that the new lesbo look?"

"Piss off," I shot back. I pushed my bowl away and hopped off the stool. "I'm leaving."

"Wait," Scott said. "Don't listen to him."

Of course, Russ wasn't the real reason I wanted to leave. He just provided the perfect excuse.

At the door Scott asked, "What are you doing tomorrow?"

"I don't know. Nothing."

"We should skate," he said. "Go to that park Russ was telling me about."

"Newport?"

"Yeah, that one."

It was tempting. I was curious about what he could do on a board, and I wouldn't mind an opportunity to show off my own killer moves. I wondered if Katja could nail a backside pivot fakie, or if she skated at all.

"Say yes," Scott said. "I promise we'll have a lot of fun."

That, I thought, *is exactly what I'm afraid of.*

And yet I agreed to meet him at Russ's place around nine the next day. He responded with a thousand-watt smile, which made me feel even more confused. Scott reminded me to bring my helmet and pads, and I promised I would.

I was almost through the door when he asked, "How much have you saved up for that new board?"

"Not much," I admitted.

"Can you get at least fifty by tomorrow?"

"I don't know—why?"

" 'Cause I think it's time we built you a new one. In the meantime, leave this one here and I'll see if I can salvage anything from it, okay?"

I walked home, half dazed. Now that I'd left my board with him, there was no way I could flake out on our skate plans. And then there was the money thing. I didn't actually have any saved, and I had no idea where I was going to get that kind of cash so quickly. The only person I could possibly ask was Jesse, and he was pretty tightfisted. But how could I pass up the chance to have a custom-made, virgin board? Even if the guy who offered to make it was only interested in hanging out with me because he'd had his heart stomped on by some girl named Katja?

The answer was, I couldn't.

It was just before eleven, and Jesse wouldn't be home until four. This left me five hours to figure out how to convince him to cough up the dough. Under normal circumstances, I'd go to Critter and ask him to help me cook up a plan. But these were not normal circumstances.

For the first time in a long, long while, I was on my own.

critter

Infatuation

I was fairly relieved when Sea took off on her own. She was wearing some two-sizes-too-small T-shirt, practically forcing my eyes to home in on "the girls," and all I could think was *I'm going to turn into a pillar of salt.*

But then I realized that everyone else was at work, and that the only other summer-school loser I knew had just abandoned me. Boredom wasted no time setting in.

It was the perfect time to call Sarah. Except, of course, she was probably at work, too. Or was she? I picked up the cordless and dialed her number. She answered after three rings.

"Hold on a second," she said, instead of hello. Then there was a long period of silence, followed by "Okay, I'm back. Who is this?"

"It's Critter," I said. "Are you busy?"

"Hey! Not really—I was just testing the water."

"Water?"

"Duh. I'm at work. You called my cell?"

"Right, right." More silence. "If this is a bad time, I could call you later."

"No," she said, "it's the perfect time. I'm so totally bored right now."

"Yeah? Me too."

"Too bad you're not here. We could, you know, entertain each other."

Alrighty then. "So when are we hanging out?"

"Hanging out, or going out? Because I thought we already had this discussion."

Her voice was playful, so I pressed on. "I'm just talking about food and a film. But you can call it whatever you want."

She laughed. "You're not going to stop until I say yes, right?"

"Would you want it any other way?"

When she didn't respond immediately, I thought I'd overplayed my hand. Then she said, "I get off at five tomorrow. You want to meet me here?"

"Sounds good," I said.

"Then it's settled," she said. "Look, I've got to get going. But I've been meaning to ask you something."

"Shoot."

"Why do they call you *Critter*?"

"Jesse had some speech problems when he was little," I explained. "For some reason, it stuck. My real name's Christopher, but now no one ever calls me that."

"Okay, then, *Christopher*," she said. "I'll see you tomorrow."

People Get Ready

I'd barely hung up the phone when Layla walked through the door.

"Hello, my darling mother," I said, and planted a kiss on her cheek.

"Hey, Boo." Her voice was flat and she sounded more tired than usual.

"What's going on?" I asked. "I thought you were working until six."

She didn't answer right away, and the longer the pause got, the more I worried about what she was about to say. Her eyes looked weary, but that wasn't anything new. I was more concerned about the way she was frowning. She pulled her hair up into her hands, ponytail-style, and then knotted it so it was off her face. Finally, she sighed and said, "You might want to sit down."

I sat.

"Frank called."

"Huh?"

"Frank," she repeated.

It took me a couple of shakes before it sunk in. "Frank *Aiken*?" I said. "Your ex-asshole?"

She nodded.

"When?"

"A couple of weeks ago. You kids were still in school."

I couldn't believe it. "You're just telling me now?"

"He called again today," she explained. "At the hospital."

"What the hell does he want? Money?"

"He's here," she said. "Well, he's in Dover. Been back a month, actually."

"How did he even get our number?"

"He's always had it," she said. "I thought he should . . . in case he needed to get in touch with Sea."

I rolled my eyes. "Like he ever would."

"Well, now, he just did."

When Sea's dad walked out on us six years ago, we weren't sure if he'd ever return. Jesse was convinced that Frank would come back eventually and want to take Sea away from us. He was like eight or nine at the time and started having body-snatcher nightmares that got so bad, Layla hauled him in to a shrink.

But when the shrink heard about our situation, she suggested that Layla bring all of us for a few sessions, to "cope with the loss of a parental unit." So Layla did, but in the first session, the shrink started leaning into Seattle, wanting her to talk about what it was like never knowing her biological mom, how she felt about her dad being gone. The woman had black hair streaked with silver, and the meanest eyes this side of a Marvel comic, and her questions made Sea squirm so bad she peed herself, right there in the shrink's office. She was so traumatized by the experience that Layla pulled us all out of therapy right quick, figuring she could deal with the situation better herself. No surprise that none of us were big fans of head-shrinking. Especially not Sea, who hadn't mentioned her real mom since.

Eventually it became abundantly clear that the bastard wasn't coming back for anything, not even his daughter. I thought that was the best possible thing for all of us. Frank had had his moments at the beginning. But mostly what I remembered were those last few months, when he started spending all of his time—and Layla's money—at the track. That and how, after he left, we lost the house and Layla lost her spark.

She had to work a lot to keep us afloat, and we never did have a shitload of money (thank you, Frank!). But she was a damn fine mother, and she never treated Seattle as anything less than her very own flesh. We had a lot of love for each other, and that was more than I could say for some families who supposedly had it made.

"He wants to see her, Boo."

Layla's voice sliced through me, and I felt the makings of another headache. "Tell him he can't," I said, my voice flat as cardboard.

"No can do," she replied. "He's her daddy; he's got rights."

"He gave up those rights when he *abandoned* her six years ago, didn't he? Screw that—screw *him*!"

"Look, I'm not saying I'm happy about this, but technically, I don't even have custody of Sea. If Frank wants to see her as badly as he says he does and I try to stop him, he could always haul my ass into court. So, we're going to have to play the game by his rules. At least for now."

Suddenly I felt the same fear I had when Jesse was having the body-snatching nightmares. Sea had been ours for so long I forgot she officially belonged to someone else—someone who could take her away from us, if he really wanted. A sick feeling snuck into my anger, and I slumped down into the cushions of the couch.

"Critter, baby," Layla cooed. "You're forgetting what kind of man Frank is. Odds are he wants to see Seattle to get rid of some guilt, and then he'll be on his way. This is nothing. This is a dog and pony show."

"Yeah, well, that dog and pony show's gonna mess with Sea's head good."

"There's nothing we can do about it," she said.

"When Sea gets home, I'll have a talk with her. Maybe I can convince her that grabbing a meal with him's the best thing she could do right now."

"Best for who, Mom?" I asked. "Because you can't tell me it's the best thing for her."

Layla patted the side of my face. "In the long run, it is. When Frank sees how well she's doing without him, he'll let her stay. But if we lock her up in the tower, he's going to storm the castle until he breaks through the doors. Nothing makes people want something more than being told they can't have it." She paused. "He is still her father, Boo. I don't know . . . maybe he really does want to do right by her."

I looked up at her. "Who are you trying to convince here, me or you?"

She didn't answer.

Try a Little Tenderness

Layla had cleared her schedule for the whole day and night. Her plan was that we'd all go out to dinner together—a rare treat—and then afterward she'd sit

Seattle down and tell her about Frank. In the meantime, she asked me not to say a word to anyone.

There had only been a handful of times that Sea had talked about Frank in the years since he'd left, and then it was mostly to say things like "If I never see that loser again, it'll be too soon." Even so, the look on her face always said something different. I kind of knew how she felt. I barely remembered my own dad, an auto mechanic/wannabe rocker who took off for L.A. long before Jesse's first birthday. As a kid, I couldn't help hoping that one day he'd get his shit together and come back. The dream died nearly a decade ago, when Layla heard from one of his former bandmates that Dad had OD'd. He'd been a loser right up until the end.

Layla headed up for a nap; not five minutes later I heard the front door squeak open slowly, like someone was trying to sneak in. *Sea*. She stopped dead when she saw me. The whole left side of her body was pitted by dark red gaping wounds, some of which had crusted over with blood.

"What the hell happened to you?"

Sea shrugged. "I told you I was going skating."

"So where's your board?" I asked.

"I left it with Scott."

"Scott?"

"You know," she said. "That guy that you . . . ran into. Yesterday."

Ah. "Who is he, anyway?"

"Russ Louten's cousin."

"Russ Louten has a cousin?"

"He's not from here," she explained. "He's visiting for the summer. From . . . Seattle." She looked almost embarrassed.

"Aw," I said. "Isn't that cute? Your new boyfriend lives in the city you were named after."

"He's *not* my boyfriend," she said hotly.

"No? Then what is he?"

"He's a skater," she said, like I'd just asked the most ridiculous question. "He builds his own boards. Said he'd take a look at mine."

"I'm sure that's not all he wants to get a look at," I muttered, sitting up.

"We're *friends*," she said. "Just because *you* want to get into your Penn Acres princess's panties doesn't mean that all guys are pigs."

"You've got to be kidding me." I sprung off the couch. "I saw you, remember? Getting dressed afterwards?"

Seattle rolled her eyes. "Nothing happened. You made quite sure of that."

"Did you honestly *want* something to happen?"

"That's none of your business," she said, her voice high and almost shrill. "Believe me, you've done way worse things with Shelli—and in public, no less."

"That's different."

"Why?" she demanded.

"It's not real," I said. But even I knew that was lame.

"Drop the dad routine, okay? That's Jesse's job."

The word "dad" echoed in my ears. So when Sea tried to stomp upstairs, I stopped her.

"I'm sorry," I said. "I don't want to fight with you."

"Then stop acting like an ass."

"If you stop acting like a . . ." I wanted to say *slut*, but I didn't. "Fine. Just . . ."

"Just what?"

"Watch yourself," I said, touching her non-scabby arm. "Guys really are pigs."

She shook my hand off and said, "You would know, wouldn't you?"

I stood frozen at the bottom of the steps until I heard her bedroom door slam shut. Then, focusing all of my frustration on my fist, I slammed it into the wall.

The wall remained intact, but my knuckles popped under the pressure. I swore under my breath, rubbing the pain and praying there'd be no bruising. No matter how intense the drama got at home, nothing would keep me from seeing Sarah the next night.

Nothing.

I'm Gonna Move to the Outskirts of Town

Layla resurfaced from her nap around six and told us we had twenty minutes to clean up for dinner. So of course it wasn't until *forty* minutes later that we all piled into the Cougar. I took shotgun, partially because of my extra-long legs and partially because I didn't want to have to deal with Sea. Things were going to be awkward enough once Layla told her about Frank—not to mention what might happen when she found out about me and Sarah's date-type thing.

"I'm craving Italian," Layla declared. "How does the Olive Garden sound?"

"Ooh, fancy," Jesse joked.

So we drove up to the one on Concord Pike, which was pretty packed for a Thursday night. It was so crowded that we not only had to wait an hour to be seated, we had to do the waiting outside in the hot, sticky air. Jesse had convinced me to trade my cutoffs for a pair of carpenter pants before we left, and the extra fabric felt itchy against my skin. Seattle, looking incredibly sour, took off for the bathroom. Layla sat down on an empty wrought iron bench and motioned for me and Jess to sit beside her, which we did. She stretched her arms around our shoulders. "My boys," she said, smiling. "How'd I get so lucky to have you?"

Jesse's eyebrows were all scrunched up. "Are you going to tell us you have some sort of disease or something?"

"No, why?"

"You're being all touchy-feely. What's the occasion?"

Layla withdrew her arms and pressed her hands to her chest in mock shock. "Do I need a reason to take my family out to a nice dinner? When did it become against the law to show a little love?"

But when Jess wasn't looking, Layla and I exchanged glances; it would make sense to Jesse soon enough.

It took Sea more than twenty minutes to return. "Did you fall in?" Jesse said. Old-man humor was his specialty. I expected her to tell him to shut up, but instead she laughed—a plastic laugh that sounded really weird coming from her mouth. "Can I talk to you for a sec? *Alone,*" she said, glaring at me.

"Sure," Jesse said. "What's up?"

How childish. At least I had the decency to keep Jess out of Sea's and my business. The two of them wandered toward Red Lobster, which sat at the far right end of Restaurant Row. "What's with the secret meeting?" Layla asked.

"Got me."

Her eyes narrowed. "You said something, didn't you?"

I shook my head. "I gave you my word, remember?"

"Sorry," she said. "I'm a little on edge."

"Understandable."

Another ten minutes went by before Jess and Sea returned, and then she wore a beaming smile. She even had her non-scabby arm linked through Jesse's. I made eyes at him, trying to ask questions without saying anything, but Jesse just shrugged. Whatever she had wanted to talk to him about must not have been that big a deal—at least not to him. Still, the not-knowing ate at me. Sea and I never kept secrets from each other. Except—

Between Sarah and Frank—not to mention my shower incident—I suddenly had several of them.

Two hours, four all-you-can-eat pasta dinners, and an infinite amount of tension later, we toddled out of the restaurant, stuffed to near explosion. I felt sick, but I doubted it had much to do with overeating. Layla still hadn't told Seattle about Frank, and the waiting was making me feel pukey.

On the way home, Layla pulled into the Charcoal Pit's parking lot. "Who's up for ice cream?"

"Funny, Mom," Jesse said.

"No," she said. "I'm serious. Let's get a Kitchen Sink and we'll all split it."

Even if I hadn't just ingested ten pounds of fettuccini, the last thing I'd want was to order the Kitchen Sink. I guess you could call it a sundae, except it arrived in a bowl big enough to hold a twenty-pound turkey—mounds upon mounds of ice cream, chocolate, crushed fruit, wet nuts, whipped cream, and maraschino cherries. Eight people couldn't finish the whole thing, let alone four.

But I knew what Layla was doing. Postponing the

conversation she needed to have with Seattle. So I did the good-son bit and said, "Sounds great, Mom!" I unbuckled my seat belt and practically skipped to the front of the restaurant.

There was another wait, almost as long as the one at the Olive Garden. Sea kept saying, "I'm not even hungry. Can't we just go home?" But clearly home was the last place Layla wanted to be, so I put my arm around my mother's shoulder and kept my mouth shut.

Eventually a skinny blonde named Jennifer seated us at a teeny tiny booth. She laughed heartily when Layla placed our order. "You guys are brave," she said. "Coming right up."

In the entire history of the Charcoal Pit, there had never been four people less enthusiastic about eating ice cream than we were that night. All together, we managed to choke down about three and a half scoops and maybe two tablespoons' worth of topping. Jennifer kept buzzing by our table, asking if everything was okay. After forty minutes, the sundae was a melted mishmash and Layla raised the white flag. "Our eyes were bigger than our stomachs."

When we finally pulled up to the house, it was going on eleven. "Who left the light on in the living room?" Layla asked. We all denied responsibility. "I guess we have ghosts," she muttered. "Maybe I should ask *them* to pay the electric bill once in a while."

All I wanted was to go inside and crawl into bed. I grabbed the keys from Layla, jogged up the front step, and opened the door. I'd made it maybe four steps in when I saw him. He was seated—no, *sprawled*—on our couch, his feet up on the end cushion, like this was an everyday occurrence. Like you could find him there any day of the week.

"Frank," I said, my voice oddly steady.

He stood up from the couch and gave a half wave. I turned to Layla, unsure if this was part of her master plan, but she was a whiter shade of pale if I ever saw one.

"How?" she said to Frank.

"Spare key," he replied. "You still keep one in a plastic frog out front."

The next few seconds were a blur; Jesse and Seattle had trailed us to the door, so they were the last inside. Jesse registered Frank's presence right away, but Sea just stood there like a statue. Then she shook her head, like she was unwilling to accept what she was seeing. "Missy," Layla said, reaching out to her, but Sea jerked away. She whipped her head around wildly, seemingly scanning the entranceway, and I realized she was looking for her skateboard.

"It's with Scott," I said. "Remember?"

She nodded, turned, and ran out the door.

seattle

Negotiating the Past

I started walking, not sure where I was going, but knowing I couldn't stay there. All the food I'd eaten that night was sloshing around my maxed-out stomach. I needed a cigarette. I needed a shot of Jäger.

I needed Frank not to be in our living room.

My head was buzzing with so many unwanted thoughts that I didn't hear Critter and Jesse approaching; I just felt Critter's hand reach for mine—the same one Scott had held earlier.

"I'm sorry," he said, pulling me toward him in a hug.

My brother's long, lanky arms slipped around me, his body covering mine like a layer of skinny-boy armor. I circled my arms around his lower back and held on tightly. I was afraid that if he let go, I might float away.

I didn't know how long it had been before I realized there was a second set of hands on my back, rubbing ovals over the fabric of my tank top. Jesse's touch sent me crashing back to reality. I wiggled free, sat down on a nearby curb, and dropped my face into my hands.

They sat down, too, flanking me. But it was Critter who extended his arm again, pulling me to him in a half hug and stroking the patch of fuzz I now called hair. "What is he *doing* here, anyway?" I asked.

"Who the hell knows?" Jesse said, but Critter just looked away.

"You knew," I accused him.

"Not exactly," he said, but he wouldn't look me in the eye.

"Well, what *exactly* did you know?"

Critter sighed. "I knew he was in Dover. And that he wanted to see you. But I swear, I didn't know he'd be here tonight. I thought Layla was going to talk to you first."

Layla. Of course she'd have known. She would've been the one to tell him where we were. *How could she?*

"What else do you know?" I asked him.

He shook his head. "That's about it. Honest."

We sat there for a while, not talking. A car passed by; maybe it was his. No one wanted to get up and check.

Eventually Jesse said, "We can't stay out here forever."

"Oh, yeah?" I said. "Watch me."

All of a sudden, Layla was walking toward us, telling the boys to go back in the house. Jesse got up right away, but Critter looked at me, waiting for approval. I nodded.

"You sure?" he asked.

"Yeah," I said. "It's okay."

Layla stood over me, her arms folded across her stomach, one foot pressing against the curb. "I am so sorry this happened the way it did. We'd agreed that I'd talk to you first. That's what tonight was supposed to be—me telling you about his call."

"How *could* you?" I shook my head. "You know how I feel about this. You know I never wanted to see him again."

"Missy, I had no idea he was going to show up like this. I swear to you."

"So?" I said. "He shouldn't have known how to find us to begin with!"

Layla sat down beside me. "You can't hide from him forever, Sea. He's your dad, and believe it or not, he loves you a lot."

"If *you* loved me, you never would've let him in our house."

I heard her draw a deep breath, sucking the air through her teeth. Then she exhaled all slow-like. Meditation breathing. After a while she said, "Listen, Missy, you don't know the whole story."

"I know enough."

"No," she said. "You don't."

I sat quietly, waiting for her to go on. She pulled her long black hair over one shoulder, separated it into three chunks, and braided it. "Well?" I finally said. "What is it you think I don't know?"

"Your dad had some problems. Things he wants to talk to you about—things we all should've talked about a long time ago. But he's not here to get you. It's not his plan to take you away from us."

I should've been relieved. That was what I wanted,

right? To stay there with her and Critter and Jesse. The thing was, once the words were spoken, I sort of wanted her to take them back.

"What if I don't want to talk to him?"

"No one will force you to," she said. "But I think you should. It's been a long time, and I think he's really trying to change. I don't mean he's going to be Ward Cleaver all of a sudden. But he seems genuinely concerned about you, about what you've been up to and if you're okay."

"I don't care what he wants," I said. "I've been doing just fine without him."

Layla nodded, her fingers undoing the braid she'd just woven in her hair. "There was a thing on *Oprah* a while back that I caught one day during rounds. She was interviewing some guy who'd written a book about fathers. A lot of it was nonsense, but one thing stuck with me. He said, 'Kids have a hole in their soul that's shaped like their dads.' "

"So?"

"So I guess what I'm trying to say," she continued, "is that I don't want you to grow up with that kind of hole. Give him a chance, Seattle. Talk to him. And after that, if you still don't want to see him anymore, I'll let it go. Okay?"

On some level, I knew she was right. One conversation wouldn't kill me. But I didn't want her to be right. I had no idea what my father had come back to say, or if I'd even want to hear his words. For all he'd known, I could've ended up in foster care, rented out to parents looking for an extra income. That hadn't stopped him from leaving.

And yet . . .

No matter how hot my anger ran, deep down I knew Layla would never ask me to do something that would really be bad for me. She was the only adult who loved me the way a parent was supposed to, who put my welfare before even her own.

"Fine," I said. "I'll have your little talk. But not tonight. Tomorrow. And not at the house, either. I want to go somewhere public. Like a restaurant or something."

"Yeah, okay," Layla said, placing her hand on my knee. "I'll even get Trish to cover for me at work, if you want, so I can be here when you get back."

"Good."

By the time we hit the front door, I was numb. Completely, totally, utterly numb. I walked past the living room and straight up the stairs. Jess and Critter were waiting for me in the bedroom. They started grilling me, trying to figure out what Layla and I had talked about. I gave them one-word answers for all of two minutes before informing them that what I really wanted was to crawl in bed and go to sleep, and that if they didn't leave me alone, I'd go nuclear.

That shut them up pretty quick.

But once they left, I couldn't fall asleep. Not right away. I felt like everything was coming undone. Why was Frank here? What did he want? I remembered something he'd said when I was really little, before he'd even met Layla. I'd been asking him why I didn't have a mom, and he'd told me she was too good for this world—that God had wanted her for his own. Then he said, "But you don't have anything to worry about, Princess. I will always be here for you. Forever and ever and ever."

Only I guess for him, "forever" meant "until you are nine."

Breakfast of Champions

Layla woke me up early the next morning, just before seven; Frank was scheduled to pick me up at eight. It wasn't until after my shower that I noticed the note taped to my mirror. It was from Jesse, who'd already left for work, and it read:

Look in your sock drawer. Hope breakfast
isn't too painful. —J

The money. I'd forgotten about it, not to mention the fact that I was supposed to meet Scott at nine. I opened the drawer and poked around until I found the bills, two twenties and a ten, tucked into the elastic of a tube sock that had lost its mate. I couldn't believe I'd sold my soul to Jesse for the fifty bucks. At first I'd called it a loan, offered him interest on the deal. But when he asked me how I planned to pay it back, I told him I was going to get my grades up so I could get a part-time job at a skate shop in the fall.

"You're serious about this?" he asked.

"Deadly."

"Then I'll make you a deal. If you get a B or higher in your summer school class, I'll call it even. But you have to keep it up come September, you got it? You get lazy and start pulling Cs again, and I'm gonna want my money back."

I agreed without hesitation. I'd meant what I'd said about getting a job. I didn't know why I'd never thought of it before, but a skate shop would be the

127

perfect place of employment. I'd get discounts, for one thing. I could read all the magazines and watch all the videos without spending a penny. Plus, I'd have the inside scoop on competitions and stuff. It was genius.

Time to get dressed. I put on the most obnoxious ensemble I owned: a black T-shirt with the word "bitch" written on it in pale pink letters, wide-legged tan pants that were a size too big and sat low on my hips, and my scuffed-up Doc Martens. Then I lined my eyes in electric blue, both on top and on the inside rims.

As a final touch, I buckled a silver-studded dog collar around my neck. I thought I'd look tough, but when I caught a glimpse of myself in the mirror, I realized that I looked exactly like those faux-punk kids that Critter and I always made fun of for trying too hard. I took the dog collar off, stuffed Jesse's fifty bucks into my back pocket, and headed downstairs.

●

He picked me up in a tricked-out Olds circa 1990. Its insides were pristine; it even smelled of new leather, though I knew that had to be the result of car wash air freshener and not the elephant gray seats. Everything on the dash was digital. There were even buttons on the steering wheel that controlled the radio.

We hadn't said more than three words to each other since we'd left the house, and he was the one who'd said them: "You look nice." It took an enormous amount of effort not to laugh in his face.

At the IHOP the hostess asked if we wanted a table or a booth. Frank indicated that I was the one who should make the decision, but I refused to utter a peep. Finally, he said, "Booth's fine," to which I responded, "I want a table."

Frank grimaced for a split second before the mask of Happy Dad fell back into place. It was funny watching him try to hide his annoyance. The hostess, though, just rolled her eyes, grabbed two sticky menus, and led us to a table in the way back.

I studied the menu like I was going to be quizzed on it at any second, even though I always ordered the same thing whenever we came here: Swedish pancakes, side of hash browns, and a cup of coffee with extra creamers. Even so, when Frank cleared his throat and asked, "Do you know what you want?" I shrugged.

He sighed and turned to look out the window, at the scenic parking lot view. His profile looked different somehow. His nose had a deeper slope than I'd remembered, and there were way more bruised-looking sagbags under his dull gray eyes. His skin looked sort of gray, too, like he hadn't gotten much sun in the past decade, and his hair had all of these coarse silver strands streaking through it.

Underneath it all, though, I could still see him. The guy I used to call Dad.

A waitress approached our table and introduced herself with a sugary "And how y'all doing today?" Her name was Cindie, and the *ie* was enough to make me hate her. But I was going to be as sweet as pie to anyone who wasn't my father.

So I smiled at her as I ordered, asking for an extra side of lingonberry jam, but only because I knew they charged a dollar for it. Frank ordered some egg thing with a side of scrapple. "I can't believe you still eat that crap," I said. "It always looks like dog food." He didn't respond.

A Muzak version of the Beatles' "Magical Mystery Tour" played over the restaurant's speaker system. I wanted to remember to tell Critter about it later, for the ever-growing list he kept of Great Musical Atrocities.

When the next song—this time a cover of Billy

Joel's "Allentown"—came on, I decided to speed things up.

"So what is it you have to say to me?"

Frank blinked a few times; clearly I'd caught him off guard.

"Well? What is it?"

"I don't know where to start," he said. "This . . . it's hard for me, Princess."

"Okay, first of all? Call me princess again and I am so out of here. And second of all, just say it. Whatever it is you came here to say. Spit it out."

He picked up his water and took a long gulp, crushed a few mostly melted cubes of ice between his teeth. I sat there, glaring at him, half expecting him to give me some soap-operaesque tale. But what he said was "I started seeing this shrink about a year ago. In Scranton. I was living in Scranton and I started seeing this shrink because I was depressed. I don't mean like sad; I mean like I couldn't get out of bed in the morning. That kind of depressed."

"Yeah?" I said. "So?"

He sighed. "So I was seeing this shrink, and it turns out . . . well, it turns out I'd been depressed for a while. Probably long before Val—uh, your mom—passed away. I guess you could say I wasn't real happy with the way my life turned out."

Oh, this was rich. The fire in my belly rose into my throat. "I suppose that's my fault, right?"

"No," he said. "Not at all. But—"

"But what? Did you actually think I'd feel *sorry* for you?"

"I wanted you to know *why* I left. Because it didn't have *anything* to do with you. Not a single thing. It was about me, about what I was going through. I should've handled things better."

"Of course you should have," I spat, sounding strong even though inside I was starting to shake. "But you've always been a selfish asshole."

He closed his eyes and gave a little nod. "Yeah," he said, eyes still closed. "That sounds about right."

"Well," I said. "Glad we cleared that up."

"I'm not finished."

"So get finished."

He rubbed the corner of one eye, almost like he was coaxing it to open again. "I messed up," he said. "I know it. I'm not looking for you to tell me any different. I was a horrible father. Okay? I said it. I. Was. A. Horrible. *Father.*"

"You were a nonexistent father," I said, my voice cracking on that final word. "And this breakfast is over."

I pushed back my chair and strode toward the door. If I'd stayed there another second, I would've started crying, and I'd already promised myself he wouldn't ever see me cry. I didn't even want to show him how angry I was, but the anger was clearly too much to control.

On the other side of the glass doors, a hot, dry morning smacked me in the face. It felt good, though, after the overly air-conditioned restaurant. I reached into my pants pockets to see if I had any coins for a pay phone, but all I had was Jesse's bills. It didn't matter. Layla had made good on her promise and taken the day off. I could walk to the Food-n-Stuff and call her collect.

I'd gone all of two steps when Frank came through the doors, spotted me, and jogged over. I willed my feet to work, but they were glued to the parking lot. In fact, it wasn't until Frank's hand reached out and brushed my shoulder that I could move at all.

"Don't you dare!" I screamed, not caring who else could hear. "Don't you dare touch me!"

"Keep your voice down," he begged.

I tried to get around him, but he moved with me, blocking me. "Please, Seattle," he said. "I'm here now, aren't I?"

I thought of my promise to Layla, that I'd at least hear him out. But she should've warned me. Especially if she'd known that all he wanted to do was whine. *Pity me, my life sucked, that's why I was a bad father.* Screw that.

Frank stood there, staring at me with pleading eyes, but I refused to get pulled in. Eventually I managed to say, "I want to go home." He nodded, pulled out the cloth napkin still tucked into the waistband of his jeans, and walked toward the Olds.

One Foot in Front of the Other

He didn't say anything to me as we drove back to the house. Even though the Olds had air-conditioning, I opened the window and breathed in the hot wind. As we turned onto our street, I checked the digital clock on the dash and saw that it was quarter to nine. If I didn't go inside, I could still make it to meet Scott on time. Of course, that would mean showing up without my helmet and pads. But I knew that if I went home, Layla would give me the third degree and I'd never get out of there.

Frank put the car in park but left it running. "I know you weren't expecting me to show up like this. But I want to talk to you. There are still some things I need to say."

"Whatever."

I set off in a sprint before he could stop me. It was only six blocks or so to Russ's house, but I landed on the doorstep a panting, sweaty mess.

"Running from the law?" Scott joked as he let me in.

I didn't answer; I just pushed past him so that I could get to the bathroom. I looked as gross as I felt. The sweat had melted my liner into junkie-chic smudges, a look not improved by my now red-rimmed eyes. I spotted a bar of soap next to the faucet and used it to scrub my face clean.

Scott was standing not too far from the door when I emerged, concern clouding his face. "You okay?"

"I left my gear at home," I said, ignoring him. "So I can't hit the skate park with you today."

"You didn't answer my question. Are you okay?"

"I'm fine," I snapped. "I just need to get my skateboard and then I'll be out of your hair."

Scott frowned. "Who said I want you out of my hair?"

"Look, I have to leave. Now. My brothers—they know Russ, know where he lives, and eventually someone's going to think about coming here to look for me. But I don't want to be found right now, so if you can just give me my board, I'll go."

"Hey," Scott said, rubbing my shoulder. "What's going on?"

I pushed his hand away. "Nothing you need to worry about."

"Seattle," he said. "This is exactly why I didn't want to tell you about Katja. Because now you think I'm just some asshole guy. Right? The thing is, I really do like you. A lot."

"That's your mistake," I said. "I'm not a very likable person." My voice cracked on those last few words, chased by the tears I'd held back when I was with Frank. I tried to turn away, but Scott pulled me into his arms, sort of like Critter had the night before, only different. Scott wasn't as bony, but he had a lot of hard muscle, and the weight of him against me made me feel suffocated. I wiggled out of his arms and took several steps back, trying to regain my balance.

"I'm sorry," he said. "You seemed so upset."

"I told you, I'm fine."

"Talk to me. Tell me what's wrong."

"I'm *fine*," I repeated. "Now where's my goddamned skateboard?"

Scott stood there, his face blank. "I took it apart last night. If you wait a few minutes, I can put it back together."

"Never mind," I said, pushing past Scott and out the front door.

I could hear him calling to me, but I didn't care. I had to get out of there. Alone. I wanted to be alone.

Alone was the safest place I could be.

You Got a Nerve

Layla shouldn't have made Seattle go. She never should have let the bastard back into the house—back into our *lives*. What was she thinking?

I glared at her from across the room as Frank explained what had happened. To hear him tell it, he was this misunderstood saintly father whose daughter had an unfortunate attitude problem. "She won't listen to me, Lala," he said, using his pet name for my mother. Was that how he'd talked to Sea? No wonder she'd run off.

Layla turned to me. "Where would she go?"

I shrugged, even though I was pretty sure I knew the answer.

She sighed heavily, grabbed the cordless phone, and took it into the kitchen. I figured she was calling the Sip-n-Stop, to check in with Jesse. Sure enough, she came back into the living room a minute later. "Jess says she's probably at this kid Russ's house—says you know where it is. I want you to bring her home."

"Why should I do your dirty work?" I asked.

"Don't give me any lip, Critter," she shot back. "Besides, I need to wait here in case Missy comes back on her own."

I should've let her have the last word, but staying quiet had never been a strength of mine. "If you'd have listened to me in the first place," I said in a calm, steady voice, "I wouldn't have to be chasing your daughter across the neighborhood."

Both she and Frank flinched when I said "daughter," which was exactly the response I was looking for.

●

I hadn't been to Russ Louten's house in ages. Not since the New Year's Eve party he'd hosted when I was a freshman. It wasn't a place I'd cared to go to very often.

But there I was, ringing the doorbell. Pasting on a fake smile when Russ himself answered the door.

"Christopher Carlisle," he drawled. "To what do I owe this honor?"

"I'm looking for Seattle," I said.

Russ grinned. "Yeah, I was expecting that."

"That so?"

"Well, I don't know too many guys who take kindly to strangers boffing their baby sisters."

I felt a rush of blood to my head. "What did you say?"

He cackled. "You heard me. Scooter says she's good, too. Real good. Surprised the hell out of me. Her being so butch and all."

My fist cracked Russ's jaw so hard that he lost his balance and crashed to the floor. I was leaning down to take another shot when I saw *him* in the doorway. Skater Boy. I was so busy looking his way that Russ might've popped me one, if his cousin hadn't rushed over and grabbed his arm.

"Settle down, boys," he said.

But my punch had split open Russ's bottom lip, and once he'd had a taste of blood, he could barely be restrained. I felt a little panicky. I wasn't much of a fighter. In fact, I'd never really thrown a punch before that day. Thankfully, Skater Boy did me a favor and dragged Russ back into the house, shutting the door behind them. I decided to wait on the front stoop. I figured Skater Boy knew who I was really looking for, and I was sure he'd come out once he'd gotten Russ squared away.

I figured right. He came out maybe five minutes later, asked me what he could do for me. I stood up, gave him my most menacing glare, and said, "You can tell me where my sister is, for starters."

"You just missed her. She came here to get her board and then took off." When I asked him where she was headed, he said he didn't know. "I do know she was trying to get away from you, though."

"Me? What the hell's that supposed to mean?"

He shrugged. "She was upset about something. Said one of her brothers would come looking for her here. I guess she was right."

It sounded wrong. Usually, when Sea was upset, I was the first person she ran to. I could see why she wouldn't want to go back to the house and deal with Frank, but to run away from *me*? It didn't make any sense.

"Anything else I can help you with?" Skater Boy asked.

I didn't like the smugness of his tone. It made me wish I'd decked him after all.

"Yeah," I said. "You can tell me you're not screwing my sister."

"I don't think that's any of your business, Critter."

I hated the way he said my name, like it was natural, like we were friends. I gathered some saliva and spat on the sidewalk to my left. "I think it is my business," I said. "And I better not find out that's what's going on."

"Why's that?"

" 'Cause I know you're not from around here. And if you think I'm going to let some snot-nosed skate rat break my sister's heart over a stupid summer fling, you've got another think coming."

He chuckled. "I don't think you have to worry about that. Your sister doesn't want anything to do with me, okay?"

"Why? What'd you do to her?"

"Oh, for Christ's sake," he said. "*Nothing* happened. I was trying to talk to her, she wigged out, and that's that. So why don't you take your drama somewhere else?"

There was something about the way he spoke that made me think there was truth in his words. Russ's trash talking was probably just that—*trash*. Still, I said, "You'd better not give me anything to worry about," which I'd meant to sound tough but which came out as more of a whine.

Even so, I couldn't help smiling as I walked away. If Skater Boy really had slept with Sea, he would've either boasted about the conquest or denied it so strongly I'd know he was lying. I was reasonably certain he hadn't been scoring any home runs on Seattle's field. I felt relieved, but it wasn't until I reached the Sip-n-Stop that I bothered to ask myself why.

●

Jesse was ringing up a string of customers when I got to the store. One of his rules was that we couldn't talk to him until his line was clear. To kill time I opened the hot dog case and helped myself to a Big-n-Juicy. I'd just finished heaping on a mess of sauerkraut when Jess finally got free.

"I take it you didn't find her," he said.

"Nope."

"Good to see your appetite hasn't been affected. Do you even have money for that?"

"Add it to my tab," I said through a mouthful of kraut.

He snorted. "Like you'll ever settle up."

"Speaking of," I began, "I need to borrow some money. I've got a date." I punctuated this sentence by cramming the remainder of the Big-n-Juicy into my mouth.

"With who? The girl from the pool?"

"Her name's Sarah," I said. I filled him in on most of the details. "Don't tell Sea, okay?"

"Why not?"

"For some reason Sea hates her. I mean, *hates her*. And she doesn't need any more stress, especially not now."

Jesse nodded. "I hear you."

"We're doing dinner and a movie. Forty should cover it, right?"

"Cut me a break," he replied. "I'm already a little light on cash this month." That raised my eyebrow. Jesse was never light on anything. But when I asked him why, all he'd say was "It's nothing. Forget I said anything."

Of course, this made me lay into him even more. "Saying 'it's nothing' means that there's an 'it' to begin with. So what's up?"

"Why do you care?" he asked. "It's my money."

Then I remembered. Waiting to get into the Olive Garden. Sea dragging Jesse off for a private chat. Question was, what was so important that she'd had to go to Jess for a loan? More than that, what was so important that Jesse had actually said yes?

"That's right," I bluffed. "Sea told me she was going to ask you for a little loan."

He rolled his eyes. "Nice try, genius. Why don't you use those brilliant detective skills to, I don't know, *get a job*?"

"Let me get this straight: when it comes to Sea, you're the Bank of Jesse, but when it comes to *me,* the teller is closed?"

A couple of pint-sized dorks came into the store and made a beeline for the magazine rack. Jesse eyed them suspiciously, but to me he said, "It's different. She actually intends to pay me back."

"With what money?"

"Well, Christopher," he said dryly, "our little girl has grown up. She's decided it's time she got her act together and entered the working world. Now that I think about it, you could take a lesson from her. I mean, really. What are you going to do when your partner in slackerdom starts working at the skate shop and leaves you eating her dust?"

I didn't know what he was talking about, and that pissed me off far more than his refusal to float me the forty. Now I was determined to find Sea, make her tell me what was going on if nothing else. As if he could read my mind, Jesse said, "Did you check the park yet?"

"What?"

"The park," he repeated. "That kiddie park, with the merry-go-round? You might find Seattle there."

"Why would she be at the park?"

"Because," Jesse said patiently, "that's where she met that Scott guy."

"Yeah, but I just saw him. He said she went there to get her skateboard and that's it. I don't think she's talking to *him*, either."

Jesse frowned. "You should check the park anyway. I don't know what's going on between her and Scott, but if she met him at the park, it means she's been hanging out there, right?"

"Good point."

"Seriously, Critter," he continued. "You need to find her. I don't care what she says, she's got to be wigged that Frank is back in town. Hell, I barely slept last night."

"Yeah. Me too."

Just before I reached the door, Jesse called out, "Will thirty hold you? I should be home by four. I can give it to you then."

Once again, he'd come through for me. "Thanks, dude. You rock."

"Just . . . go find her."

"Will do."

seattle

Swinging Low

I'd been "hiding out" on the swing set for what felt like a really long time when I saw him heading into the park. His hands were shoved deep in his pockets, and his lips were curled slightly in a soft, friendly smile. I hated to admit it, but I was glad to see him coming toward me.

Scott.

"How did you know where I was?" I asked.

He shrugged. "Educated guess?"

A normal girl would've had the right response on the tip of her tongue. Something smart and flirty that didn't sound like she was trying too hard. Of course, I'd never been a normal girl. That meant I said absolutely nothing. I was nearly suffocating on the silence when he tossed me a bone: "You want a push?"

"Huh?"

"On the swing," he said. "You want a push?"

"Nah," I said. "I'm okay."

"C'mon, you know you want it."

Scott slipped behind me. When he grasped the bottom of the chain, his knuckles brushed my butt and made my heart beat extra fast. He stepped back, pulling me with him, and then gave me a mighty shove. Before I rebounded, he'd run clear under me and out to the other side. I pumped my legs a few times before I started to feel self-conscious, what with Scott staring at me the whole time.

When the swing slowed, I jumped off and landed all of six inches from his feet.

"Why did you stop?" he asked.

"You know why."

I wasn't talking about the swing, though. One

look into his steel blue eyes let me know that he wasn't either.

"We don't have to stop," he said softly, moving even closer to me. Without another word, he pulled his hands from his pockets and cupped them around my face. Our noses were almost touching when I heard him say, "Open your eyes."

"Why?"

"I want to kiss you," Scott said. "But only if your eyes are open."

My heart thumped hard in my chest. If I did what he asked, I'd be opening more than my eyes. And yet I couldn't stop them; they opened like they had a mind of their own.

"Better," he said.

In the movies women are always talking about how a good kiss left them weak in the knees. I'd always thought it was a stupid thing to say—until that moment. The last time Scott had kissed me, I was wearing little more than a turquoise bra, but it was the whole kissing-with-our-eyes-open thing that really made me feel naked.

I don't know what made me pull away from a kiss that good. Maybe I could feel we were being watched.

Because when I broke the kiss and turned, Critter was standing there staring at us, not even a pool-length away. Our eyes locked for only a split second, but it was long enough for me to feel like I was caught doing something wrong. He shook his head in disgust, turned, and walked away.

"Was that your brother?" Scott asked.

I nodded.

"He came by earlier. Looking for you."

It didn't surprise me. "I told you he would."

"Yeah, but you still haven't told me *why.*"

I chewed on my top lip, wondering how much I should say, or if I should say anything at all. This was family business, and Scott wasn't family. Telling him about my deadbeat dad would feel even more personal than that kiss.

"Never mind," Scott said, interrupting my thoughts. "You'll tell me when you're ready." He held out his hand, but I didn't take it, not right away. He waited patiently, and then, still holding it out, he said, "We haven't got all day."

"What do you mean?"

"We've got plans, remember?" His voice was light, happy. "Let's go build you a new skateboard."

Kinetic Connection

We took Russ's mom's car—a white Ford Escort with her name, Amy, airbrushed in purple on the license plate frame—up 202 North to this small shopping center near the Pennsylvania state line. Sandwiched between the India Grille and a blinds store was Kinetic Skateboarding—a pretty lame name for a skate shop, but at least it was cool inside. The front end held rack after rack of sneakers, T-shirts, and hats. The right and back walls sported decks of every size and color. My eyes zeroed in on this wicked lime green Popwar model with flickery white flames screened over it. Such a beauty. Scott saw me drooling and whispered, "Look but don't touch."

"Meanie."

He headed up to the counter and asked for Brannon, who was the owner or manager or something. The guy who came out from the back looked way too prep to be a good skater, but then again, Scott didn't look so punk himself, and he knew tons.

Scott introduced himself and said, "My buddy

Oakland was supposed to give you a call about a favor I needed."

"Right, right," Brannon said. "You're the kid from Seattle."

"That's me."

They did some weird guy handshake thing I couldn't follow. Then Brannon said, "I've got your stuff in the back," and disappeared through a door situated between two racks of decks. I dug into my pocket and pulled out the money Jesse had left me.

"There's fifty," I said. "It's all I could get."

Scott took the bills and said, "Go get some grip tape. Shorty's Black Magic."

When I got back, Brannon was showing Scott the deck he'd gotten from the back room. It was completely blank, without even a base coat of paint on it. "We don't usually sell without a logo," Brannon said, "but Oak told me you needed cheap."

"Take a look," Scott said, handing me the deck. "It's shorter than your old one and a little less wide, which should help you with your tricks. Plus, it's seven-ply, instead of five, so it should give you tons more pop."

I ran my hand along the smooth Canadian maple. My Kryptonics was only the second skateboard I'd owned, and I'd bought it used at the Farmer's Market two summers before. I'd never had the luxury of owning a virgin deck, let alone one I'd made myself.

We left the deck on the counter while Scott took me around the store, pulling the rest of the stuff he thought I should buy. "I think we should go with the Venture trucks. The Superlights only last about a year, but they're going to give you what you want, and you can always upgrade later." To that he added the wheels—Spitfire Classics in a green and black swirl that were small and hard and absolutely perfect.

What wasn't perfect was the price tag on this little shopping excursion: $82.97. Scott shook his head and said, "No can do. We only have fifty," but Brannon didn't want to budge. "C'mon," Scott said, "can't you help out a friend of a friend?"

They went back and forth for a bit and eventually Brannon came down to seventy, grumbling about how he was losing money on the deal. Thank God Delaware doesn't have any sales tax.

Scott said, "How about I kick in ten of my own? That would give you sixty."

"Sixty?" Brannon said. "What have you been smoking?"

Scott chuckled. "What's an extra ten bucks between friends?"

"You," Brannon said, "are no friend of mine." He sighed. "Okay, okay. Sixty. But you tell Oakland we're square—no, you tell him that *he* owes *me* now."

Watching Scott negotiate on my behalf was sort of hot, even though I wasn't totally comfortable with him putting in any of his own money. As Brannon rang up the purchase, I whispered, "I'll pay you back."

"No biggie."

The store had this really rank smell—like sweat and sawdust and burnt sugar all rolled into one—and I got a big whiff as we headed out the door. I must've made a face, because Scott said, "It's curry."

"What's curry?"

"What you're smelling. It's from the Indian place next door."

"Is that, like, some kind of animal?"

He laughed. "It's a spice. You've never eaten curry before?"

"No."

"Then you're in for a treat."

Next door looked too fancy for what I was wearing, but Scott said I was being silly—that I'd look pretty even if I was wearing a garbage bag. I wanted to believe him, but I felt horribly self-conscious when the hostess, who was sporting some gorgeous silk wrap thing, seated us. The menus were huge and didn't make any sense to me, so I told Scott he should order for us both. He asked me if I was allergic to anything (broccoli) and if I could handle spicy (medium). He reeled off a list of items to the bow-tied waiter, and after he finished I said, "You just gave all of my money to Brannon."

"Don't worry," he said. "It's on me."

Every time I blinked, the waiter brought out more food—hot, puffy bread; triangular dough things filled with meat and potatoes; steamy platters of rice; creamy orange goop topped with nuts; green goop mixed with whitish chunks; and something resembling chicken that was drowning in a dull yellow (curry) sauce.

"I don't know if I can eat all this," I told him when the waiter had gone.

"Just try it," he said. "I promise I won't poison you."

I grimaced as he filled my plate. But suddenly I felt very, very hungry, so I took a few tentative bites. He was right; it *was* good.

Scott couldn't stop smiling at me, like he was happy just watching me eat. It was nice, him looking at me like that. But it also made me feel guilty about how I'd acted before. He wasn't a bad guy; he was just someone's ex-boyfriend. That didn't mean I couldn't trust him.

I smooshed some of the green chunky stuff into a circle, took a deep breath, and said, "Remember when you asked me what was wrong and I wouldn't tell you? Well, I had breakfast with my dad."

"And you guys had some kind of fight?"

I shook my head. "It's sort of bigger than that." I explained about him leaving and then showing up so unexpectedly, wanting me to act like he hadn't been gone all that time. "Anyway, it's a big mess, but the point is now he's decided he wants to play daddy, and all I want is for him to go the hell away."

"That's . . . harsh."

"Harsh? No, that's *normal*. What's harsh is abandoning your daughter for six years and not calling or writing or even—"

"Calm down," Scott interjected. "I didn't mean *you* were being harsh. I meant the situation was harsh. That's all."

I felt stupid, defensive. I mumbled an apology.

"Hey, it's okay," he said. "I can take it."

But clearly I couldn't, because that's when they

snuck up on me again. Tears. Big, fat, salty ones, filling up my eyes and pouring down my flaming-hot cheeks. Thankfully, Scott didn't say a word; he just handed me his cloth napkin.

"I don't know what's wrong with me," I said, trying to sniff it all back in. "I hate him. I mean, I really, really hate him. But at the same time, all I can think is *What took you so long?*"

critter

Days of Rage

I couldn't stop playing the scene over and over in my head. Skater Boy clutching Sea in the park, their lips locked, his big stupid hands groping her in places she shouldn't be groped. Not even an hour after he'd told me point-blank that she didn't want anything to do with him anymore, that he was just trying to talk her out of some meltdown. *Right.*

"Well?" Layla demanded after I'd stormed into the house. "Did you find her?"

I snorted my response.

"Damn it, Critter, I don't have time for your games."

I grabbed the plastic quart of milk from the fridge and took a swig. "Yeah, I found her. She was with her new boyfriend."

Layla's forehead wrinkled in confusion. "Boyfriend?"

"Boyfriend," I confirmed. "This loser kid's cousin. I caught them in her bed a couple days ago. Sea was half naked. You might want to give her the birds-and-bees routine, if you haven't already."

Her mouth was open so wide you could've fit a goose egg in it. I couldn't help feeling a rush of satisfaction. Sea was in a heap of trouble now. Frank or no Frank, there's no way Layla would tolerate her only daughter getting jiggy with some horny out-of-towner.

I gave her my best stab at a smug smile and chased it with another swig of milk. Next thing I knew, Layla's open palm connected with the base of the jug, sending it to the floor and creamy white spatters across every surface—including me.

"What the hell?" I hollered.

"How dare you," she said, her voice a low growl. "I work fourteen-hour days to keep the three of you fed, clothed, and sheltered—and this is how you repay me? With such blatant disrespect?"

I took a couple of steps backward. "Why are you yelling at me? I didn't do anything wrong!"

"Oh, really? So you think it's okay not to tell me that your sister may or may not be sleeping with her new boyfriend? A boyfriend I didn't even know existed? What the hell is going on around here? You're supposed to be focused on your studies, not your social lives. Do I need to find the three of you a goddamned *babysitter*?"

Just then Frank materialized in the kitchen. Why was he still here? And why—*why?*—was that asshole rubbing my mother's right shoulder?

"Calm down, Lala," he said soothingly. "Everything will be okay. I promise."

Anger shot up inside me. "You *promise*? Promise what? That you'll disappear for another six years and then show up out of the blue, throwing all of our lives into complete turmoil? Your promises aren't worth shit, Frank. *You* aren't worth shit. *Now get your hands off of my mother!*"

He backed away, his hands raised like he'd just been taken hostage in a bank robbery. "Now, hold up there, Critter. I'm not here to cause any trouble. That's not what I came back here for."

"So what did you come back here for, Frank?

Hmm? Taking a little guilt trip? Or are you just looking for a way back into my mother's bed?"

"Christopher!" Layla shrieked. "That's enough!"

"You're right," I said coldly. "It is."

I stormed past the two of them, went into my bedroom, and slammed the door behind me.

Debris

I'd been blaring *Gasoline Alley,* trying to shake off this morning's bullshit before my date with Sarah, when I realized my bedroom smelled like a wet, moldy gym sock. When was the last time I'd cleaned? It seemed to me that the entire contents of my closet were covering every available surface and square inch of floor. Since I needed to blow off some steam anyway, I decided to straighten up.

With the stereo volume on seven, I picked through the laundry, smelling to see what was clean and separating it from what had to be washed. In a third pile went the clothes I was ready to be rid of—underwear with frayed elastic, T-shirts with too many holes in them, socks that hadn't had partners since *Dawson's Creek* was still on TV. By the time Rod was belting out the ultra-bluesy "Cut Across Shorty," I'd managed to clear enough of a path that my navy blue carpeting was visible once again.

When I moved on to the third selection of the afternoon—*Blondes Have More Fun*—all I really had left to do was strip the bed and throw down some fresh sheets. But by the time I was done, I was a sweaty, stinky mess. Jesse hadn't come home from work yet and the house sounded dead quiet, like I was the only one in it.

My plan was to take a quick shower, get dressed, and ride the DART buses up to North Wilmington. I'd also thought about stopping along the way to buy Sarah some flowers. She seemed like the kind of girl who'd like that.

Everything was going smoothly until I headed downstairs and saw Layla's keys lying on the freshly cleaned countertop, right next to her purse. I'd *thought* no one was home. I stepped out the front door, and sure enough, the Cougar was there.

Frank's Oldsmobile, though, was not.

There was no note taped to the fridge—Layla's usual spot for messages—which pissed me off even more. Without a second thought, I grabbed her purse and pulled out her wallet. All she had was two fives. That wasn't enough for dinner and a movie, so I put the fives back and took out her ATM card instead, hoping she hadn't changed the PIN recently. Then I swiped her keys, jumped into the Cougar, and took off.

I parked at the nearest ATM and asked for forty. Two twenties shot out and I shoved them into my pocket, almost forgetting to take the receipt. Almost. The balance after my unexpected withdrawal was $51.75. Since it was only the second day of the month, that meant that either Layla hadn't gotten her check on the first like she was supposed to, or she'd already spent most of it on bills. A pang of conscience stabbed at my stomach—until I remembered that she'd run off with Frank. For all I knew, she could've given *him* the money. I crumpled the receipt and shot it into a nearby trash can.

Sarah was skimming the pool when I arrived. She waved and said, "I need a few minutes. Let yourself in, okay?" I unlatched the gate with one hand and kept the daisies I'd purchased at a nearby Food-n-Stuff hidden behind my back, so I could surprise her later.

She was still in lifeguard gear, wearing a black one-piece sprinkled with little white polka dots and absolutely nothing else. No sarong, no shorts, no shoes. Her skin had turned even more golden since I'd seen her last, though I didn't know how that was possible, and now her hair had these whitish blond strands that made it look like her whole head was glowing.

Sarah put the net up, grabbed her backpack, and disappeared into the girls' bathroom. No time like the present for some minty-fresh breath! I shook a couple of Tic Tacs into my mouth. Then I worried that I'd eaten too many—that she'd smell them on my breath and think I was trying too hard—so I walked over to the fence and spit them out into the bushes on the other side. When I turned, Sarah was only a couple of feet away with an odd look on her face. "What are those?"

She'd seen the daisies.

"I brought them for you," I said, thrusting the bunch forward.

Sarah took them from me gently. "Oh. Thanks."

She seemed so uncomfortable. "Yeah," I said, trying to cover, "I stopped to get gas earlier and this guy was giving them away. You know, with a fill-up? I'm not a flowery kind of guy, so I thought you might like them."

"Oh," she said again, visibly relieved.

This was not a good sign.

We decided to take Sarah's car, since mine had no AC. Sarah threw the daisies into the backseat of her BMW without even looking at where they landed. It bothered me, but I didn't say anything. After all, I was the one who'd told her they were free.

There was a CD in the player, from one of those wounded-boy singer-songwriter types. "I love this song," Sarah said, turning up the volume. "It's awesome. You should listen to it."

But it wasn't my kind of music. There was no gut in it, no heart. The guy was like the anti-Rod—a so-called indie type who was really only one step up from prefab pop star, like all those half-naked blondes whose names I could never keep straight. Thank God Sea and Jesse didn't listen to any of that crap. I didn't love Sea's angry-girl rock or Jesse's thug-rap anthems, but at least I respected the artists they admired. This, though . . . this was a whole different kind of painful.

"What's wrong?" Sarah asked, breaking my train of thought.

"Nothing."

"Liar," she said, grinning. "You hate my music, don't you?"

"Hate's an awfully strong word."

She rolled her eyes. "Don't you, like, *worship* Rod Stewart?"

"So?" I bristled.

"So nothing," she said. "Forget I said anything."

She pulled into this place called Panera (her choice), located in the shopping center behind the movie theater. It was one of the corporate kinds of hangouts with overpriced coffee and arty light fixtures. Sarah ordered a chicken Caesar, hold the croutons, and a diet black cherry soda.

"Please tell me you're not one of *those* girls."

"To which girls are you referring?" she asked in a tight voice.

"The kind who are always on a diet, even though you can't find an ounce of fat on their entire bodies."

She shrugged. "I do South Beach," she said. "I feel *healthier* when I watch my carbs."

"Right. Healthy."

Sarah blinked at me a few times. I could tell she wanted to say more but held back. Maybe she didn't want to seem rude.

When she'd ducked into the pool's bathroom earlier, she'd pulled a pair of dark red pants over her bathing suit. They hung low on her hips and stopped mid-calf. She'd also thrown on a white short-sleeved top that she left unbuttoned, so you could see the polka-dotted suit and her flatter-than-flat stomach. On her feet—feet I'd dreamed about—were a pair of beaded flip-flops.

There I was, standing literally inches away from this really hot girl I'd been thinking about nonstop since I accidentally met her, and what do you know?

I was having a fairly shitty time.

We didn't talk much while we ate. Sarah still looked irritated about my diet comment, and I was annoyed about paying twelve dollars for a sandwich, a bag of chips, and a medium Coke. But also I couldn't shake this feeling . . . like it was Christmas morning, and I'd opened the box I'd found in the back of Mom's closet that I *thought* was the PlayStation I'd been dying for, but turned out to be something incredibly stupid or boring, like a bathrobe.

Was Sarah my bathrobe?

At the movie theater, I looked at the marquee. Out of the sixteen choices, the only ones that interested me were a Ben Stiller–Owen Wilson buddy flick, the Farrelly brothers' newest gross-out comedy, and Jackie Chan's time-traveling kung fu Western.

"So what do you want to see?" Sarah asked.

I was leaning toward Jackie Chan when I noticed that Sarah was staring at my face, waiting for me to say the wrong thing. It was a test, a setup.

I was determined not to fail.

"How about that new Julia Roberts movie?"

"Really?" she asked, surprised.

"Oh, yeah. Love her stuff."

Sarah chuckled. "I was so sure you were going to make me see that stupid Western."

"Please," I said. "Give me a little credit."

It was total BS, but whatever. I'd figured out the game and I'd won. At least this round, anyway.

The movie was crap, even worse than Sarah's whiny-boy music. But when we took our seats, Sarah slipped off her flip-flops, crossed her legs, and let her naked foot rest on my calf. My desire for her returned—literally. I kept the bucket of popcorn over my crotch to hide the evidence.

After the credits rolled, Sarah turned to me and said, "I'm not ready to go home yet. Wanna get some ice cream?" The thought of watching her work a cone made me wish I still had the protection of my popcorn bucket.

"Sure," I squeaked. "Sounds great."

We drove over the state line to this place called Brewster's. Sarah ordered a large vanilla soft serve with a chocolate dip. I braved a joke: "I hear chocolate makes everything low carb." Instead of getting mad, she laughed, poked me in my side, and said, "Oh, whatever."

The evening was definitely improving.

We took our treats around back and ate them while sitting at a wooden picnic table. The mosquitoes were out in full force, and every thirty seconds one of us was slapping them off our skin.

"So what instrument do you play?" Sarah asked, nailing a big mama trying to drink from her elbow.

"None."

She seemed surprised. "I would've sworn you were a musician. You're so . . . you know . . . *opinionated* about that sort of thing."

"I love music," I said. "Other people's music. I have zero desire to write or perform my own."

"Why's that?"

I couldn't tell her the real answer, which featured my father the junkie, so I shrugged and said, "Because then it would be too much like work."

She laughed. "What, are you allergic to work or something?"

"*No,*" I snapped.

If I'd been looking for the perfect way to kill a conversation, that would've been it. Sarah didn't say anything else; she just licked her cone and looked off into the distance. I took a long drag of my root beer float and tried to figure out why talking had come so easily at the pool—and why now it seemed like the hardest thing of all.

I looked Sarah straight in the eye. "I have to go to summer school because I failed English. *That's* why I'm not working this summer." I slapped at yet another mosquito on the back of my neck.

"So what?" she said with a shrug. "Lots of people have to go to summer school. Hell, I probably would've failed precalc if my teacher hadn't been a perv or I'd flashed him a little less leg." She grinned. "Besides, working is overrated. I prefer playtime myself."

Nice.

I was staring at the little dribbles of melted ice cream that kept falling onto her wrist when Sarah thrust the dregs of her cone at me. "You want this?"

"That's okay."

She popped up and dumped it into the trash. When she returned, she sat on the edge of the table and rested her feet next to me on the bench.

171

I chuckled. "You know, I would've pegged you as an honor student. You seem really . . . smart."

"I do okay," she said. "I could do better, though, if I cared enough. But my parents have made it clear that they'll only pay for college if I go to Delaware and live at home instead of the dorms. It's not much of an incentive."

At least your parents can afford college, I thought.

"So what about you?" Sarah asked. "Got any post-high-school plans?"

"Not really. My mom's pushing for me to go to school, but I don't know. My brother, Jesse, is the genius in the family. He can read something once and remember it forever. Me, I could read the same thing fifty times and it still wouldn't stick."

"I know what you mean," she said. "It's like my brain is this blank tape, right? I can record a bunch of stuff on it—dates, formulas, whatever—but then as soon as I've taken the test, it's gone. I never feel like I'm actually learning anything, except maybe how to take tests."

I couldn't take my eyes off her. It was as if she had morphed right before my eyes, turning back into the girl who'd told me she wanted to live in a song. I wanted to say something truly profound in response, but I had lost the ability to form complete sentences.

"So what are you doing on the Fourth?" she asked.

"I don't know," I said. "We usually end up at the Riverfront. Sea gets off on the medley they play during the fireworks—you know, all those I-heart-America tunes. Taps into her inner cheese, I suppose."

"How would you like to do something different this year?"

"What do you have in mind?" I asked, trying to suppress a grin.

She smiled. "My family hosts this massive pool party cookout every Fourth of July. They even hire caterers to set up a spit and roast a whole pig, head and all."

"Wow," I said. "Sounds gruesome."

"Yeah, I guess. So what do you think? I mean, I can't offer you a cheesy medley and fireworks, but my dad usually plays the Beach Boys' entire catalog, and my uncle Phil brings cartons of smuggled sparklers. Plus, there's the pool, and my parents don't mind if my friends have a couple beers, as long as they hand over their keys when they get to the house."

"All that and Hog-on-a-Stick? How can anyone refuse that?"

"So you'll come, then?" Her voice was sweet and clear, like honey.

I wanted to say yes—this was exactly the kind of in I'd been waiting for—but I couldn't help wondering what the crowd would be like. "Who else is going? Anyone I'd know?"

"Kristen Seltzer—she's my best friend—and most of the girls we hang out with: Jaime Black, Kate Cotillo, Erin Blair. But they go to New Castle Baptist with me, so I don't think you'd know them."

"No."

She continued to reel off names of people I'd never heard of or even run into, even though half of them were from Haley. It was a big school, but not that big. It made me feel like I'd been sleeping through the past three years.

"What about Boyfriend?" I asked, trying to sound as casual as possible.

"Duncan," she said flatly. "No. No, he's not. He was supposed to come, but apparently he's got double sessions at soccer camp. Says he can't skip out because the guys would rag on him too hard."

More trouble in paradise? The night was getting better by the second.

"Oh well," she said. "At least I know where I rank, right?"

Again, I searched for the right words, but the only thing that came out was "Okay, sure. I'll be there."

"Really?"

"Yeah, why not?"

"Excellent," she said. "You should bring your brother. I'd like to meet him. Your sister, too, if you want."

Her smile was warm, sexy. It helped me block out thoughts of the trouble I knew Sea would probably cause if she went to Sarah's party.

Sarah bent over so that her head was closer to mine, giving me a clear view down her bathing suit. What did she want from me? I'd misinterpreted so many signals from her already that I couldn't decide whether or not to make a move.

Finally, she whispered, "If I told you that I wanted you to kiss me, would you do it?"

Before I could answer, her lips had already made contact.

seattle

Nowhere to Run, Nowhere to Hide

Scott and I drove around for hours. We didn't even talk most of the time; we just listened to the radio. The music and the motion of the car were soothing, and I was grateful for the silence.

Eventually, though, we had to head back to New Castle. Scott wanted to drive me to my house, but I was worried that Layla would be sitting on the front stoop, ready to pounce. I told him I would walk home from

Russ's, but then he wanted to walk with me. Finally, I had to come right out and say it: "You can't be at my house. Not right now."

The compromise was that he'd drop me off a block away and watch from the street until I got inside. But the closer we got, the sicker I felt. There were too many people waiting for me in there, and memories I'd tried so hard to block out.

As the car idled, Scott said, "I'll need a couple days to get your board ready."

"Yeah?"

"Yeah," he said. "It'll be beautiful, though. I promise."

A surge of gratitude shot through my body. "Hey, thank you. I mean, really. Thanks."

He smiled. "Thank me when I give it to you."

Scott was stroking the side of my face, looking so deep into my eyes that I got that naked feeling again. What was wrong with me? This was the kind of moment girls were supposed to dream about, but there I was, fighting hard not to pull away.

"I'll see you later," I said, and scrambled out of the car before he could lean in for a goodnight kiss.

Why Ask Why?

I'd barely walked through the door when I heard Layla growl, *"Where the hell have you been?"*

I swallowed hard and said, "Out."

That was when all hell broke loose.

It was one of the loudest, most effective guilt trips Layla had ever delivered—a voyage spiked with obscenities that shocked even me. She screamed so hard and so long that even Jesse got alarmed; instead of weathering the storm in the shelter of our room, he came downstairs to try to calm her down. It was an unwelcome gesture. Layla shook Jesse's arm off her shoulder and shouted, "Stay out of it!" As for me, I just stood there, absorbing her wrath.

Finally, Layla was all screamed out. She sat on the bottom step and started to cry. If anyone in the world was less of a crier than me, it was Layla. Watching her lose it sent *me* over the edge again. I felt myself starting to shake, just a little at first, until all the things building inside me started to spew out:

"How can you yell at me when this is *your* fault? I

told you I didn't want to talk to him—but you *made* me! Why did you do that?" When she didn't answer, I continued, "You think you know what's best for me, but you don't. You don't know what I think. What I feel. Not when it comes to him."

She lifted her head and stared straight at me. "So why don't you tell me, then?"

"*I hate him!*" I howled. "He abandoned me—abandoned all of us. I hate him for that, and you will never make me understand why you don't hate him too. For Christ's sake, Layla, all you've done for the past six years is take care of his mistakes—me included."

Jesse cut in. "Sea, stop."

"I won't," I said, never taking my eyes off Layla. "You know it's true. How many times are you going to let this man screw us over? I don't know what's worse— you taking it from him or asking me to."

"That's not what this is about," Layla said wearily.

"All I know is that you're the reason he's here. *You.* He wouldn't even have known how to find us if you hadn't drawn him the map. And now he's here, and the two of you want me to let him play daddy— as if none of it ever happened. But I can't do that, Layla! It's not my fault he's all kinds of crazy, and it's not my fault that he didn't love me enough to stick around."

I'd barely gotten that last sentence out when I realized why Jesse had been telling me to shut up earlier.

Frank walked in from the kitchen, a bottle of beer clutched tightly in his hand. "Is that what you really think?" he asked.

I was too stunned to answer.

"I didn't come back here to play daddy. I came back because no matter how big a mess I made of my life—and trust me, it's bigger than you know—I always knew there was at least one thing I did right: you. I just wanted the chance to know you, Seattle. That's all." He handed Layla his beer. "I'm taking off now."

"Frank—no."

"This was a mistake," he said. "I shouldn't have come back here." He mumbled an apology in my direction and was out the door before I knew what had hit me.

None of us said a word, but I could feel both Layla's and Jesse's eyes glued on me, to see what I might do or say next. When I couldn't take the silence any longer, I said, "Well, I'm glad that's finally over." Then I ran up to my room, locked the door behind me, and cried myself senseless.

critter

Crazy About Her

Sarah dropped me off at my car around twelve-thirty, and we kissed a little more before saying good night.

"I probably won't get to talk to you before Sunday," she said. "It's going to be pretty crazy the next few days, helping my parents get ready for the party and all."

"Sure," I said. "I won't take it personally."

What I did take personally was the kissing, which was beyond hot. So much for Duncan Mackenzie. I had a feeling she'd be dropping his jock ass the first chance she got.

Driving home, I listened to Lynyrd Skynyrd on the eight-track, singing "Simple Man" at the top of my lungs. Everything was falling into place with Sarah and it felt *amazing*. So amazing that I'd forgotten to worry about the fact that I'd pretty much stolen Layla's car, not to mention her ATM card and forty bucks.

I cut the Cougar's lights as I rolled onto our street. It was after one and the house was completely dark. Hopefully that meant everyone was asleep. They were—except instead of nestling in his own bed, Jesse was sleeping soundly in mine.

It took me a few tries to get him up. When I did, he told me that Sea had locked him out of their room. Then he told me about the showdown between her, Layla, and Frank.

"But the thing that really threw her over the edge," Jesse said, "was *you*."

"Me? What did I do now?"

"Went on a date with the pool bunny."

I could've killed him.

"She figured it out," Jess explained. "When you weren't here and I was. She knew."

"Great," I said. "Beautiful."

"I tried to get her to talk, but it's not the same with me, you know? You were the one she wanted."

I nodded; we both knew it was true. "So is she okay now?"

"I don't know," he said. "Want me to see if the door's still locked?"

He did and it was. When he returned, he asked me if Sea and I had ever really talked about Frank.

"No," I said. "Not that it surprises me. I mean, you and I never talk about Dad."

"I think about him, though," Jesse said quietly. "I think about him a lot, actually."

"So how come you never said anything?"

"What's there to say? 'Gee, it really sucks that my father was a loser who ran off before I was out of diapers.' You know, when he died, I didn't feel anything. How could I? I never even knew him."

I nodded. "I didn't know him much better than you did."

"Yeah, but at least you have memories. All I've got is a single Polaroid of him holding me when I was still covered in birth slime."

"Jess, man—I had no idea."

"Whatever." He folded his arms across his chest and sighed. "Don't act like I'm all wounded. Truth is, if he hadn't run off, Mom wouldn't have hooked up with Frank, and you and I wouldn't have a sister."

"Good point."

"Not to change the subject," Jesse said, "but you're going to be in a world of hurt tomorrow."

"Because of the money?"

"No, because of the car," he said, looking confused. "What money?"

"Never mind."

"Hey," he said, punching me lightly on the shoulder. "What money? *My* money?"

I shook my head. "I took Layla's ATM card. I used it to get the money for my date."

Jesse's jaw dropped. "Why would you do that?"

"Don't start with me," I said. "You weren't here, she took off with Frank, and I needed cash."

"So you just *stole* it?"

"No. I mean, okay, *yes*. Temporarily. But I'll take the money you were going to lend me and deposit it back in tomorrow. It'll look like a bank error."

"And what if I don't lend you the money now?"

"Come on, Jess," I said. "Do you want to watch Layla lose it completely?"

He glared at me. "I already did."

"Dude, what's your problem?"

"You," he said. "I'm tired of having to take care of your sorry ass."

"Cry me a river," I shot back.

"Screw you." After some more glaring, he added, "I gotta work at six tomorrow. Since I don't have access to my own bed, I'm taking yours. You can sleep on the couch."

"What makes you think you can kick me out of *my* room?"

"Oh, I'm guessing *my* forty dollars can buy me a night's rest."

There was no point in arguing. "Fine," I said. "But make sure I have it in hand before you leave."

Once I hit the couch, I couldn't sleep. Thinking about Sarah soothed me. Everything about her was soft—her hair, her cheeks, her lips. Even her fingers were free of hangnails and paper cuts. It was like making out with a big stick of butter.

Keeping her on the brain, and forcing out thoughts of anything and anyone else, I eventually drifted off into a deep, dreamless sleep.

Hard Lesson to Learn

When I woke up the next morning, there was a note from Jesse pinned to the front of my shirt, saying that he'd take care of "it" on his mid-morning break and that I owed him "huge." In the kitchen I found another note, this one from Layla, taped to the fridge. It read "Say goodbye to your car privileges. We'll talk when I get home."

After a stretch, a yawn, and a scratch, I made breakfast: untoasted strawberry-flavored Pop-Tarts and a mug of Coke. As I ate, I thought about Sarah's party. After what Jesse had told me, I knew there was no way I could bring Sea with me. I had a feeling this party would be my audition for a full-access pass to Sarah World, and I couldn't let anything jeopardize that.

But I couldn't *not* invite her, either. Not when she and Jess and I always spent the Fourth together. Layla too, when she wasn't aiming for more overtime.

The only option was to make the party sound as stiff, formal, and dull as possible—make her an offer she would *want* to refuse.

Sea wandered in a little while later. "Hey," she said sleepily. "I wasn't sure you'd be here."

I let the comment slide; she looked like shit and didn't need me heaping on any more. "How are you doing?" I asked. "Jesse told me what went down last night and—"

"I don't want to talk about it."

"Okay."

She grabbed two more packets of Pop-Tarts from the cupboard and tossed me one. "There is something I want to talk to you about, though."

"Yeah?"

"I think I might ask Scott to hang out with us on Sunday. I was telling him about the fireworks at the Riverfront, and how much fun we usually have there, and it seemed like maybe he'd want to go."

Score!

"That's cool," I said. "Sarah's invited us all to a party that night, but I think it's going to be lame. Her dad's a dentist, and you know how boring those dentist types are."

"Hmm."

"Plus," I continued, dunking a piece of Pop-Tart into my Coke, "I think it's a dry party. No alcohol or

187

anything." She shrugged, and I pressed on. "I think Scott would like the Riverfront, though. Especially the fireworks. There won't be any of those at Sarah's party."

Another shrug.

"Yeah, it's going to be a total drag," I said, wondering if I sounded half as desperate as I felt. "I mean, I *have* to go. She really, really wants me there. But there's no reason you guys can't have a fun Fourth without me."

"If I didn't know any better," Seattle said, "I'd think that you didn't want us at your girlfriend's little get-together."

"Why would you say that?" I asked in my Mr. Innocent voice.

"Oh, cut the crap. You don't want me there because I don't like Sarah, and you clearly don't like Scott. So fine. I won't go. Really, I have bigger things to deal with right now."

She buried her head in the fridge and I shrunk into my stool. I'd been so focused on me and Sarah that I'd practically forgotten the stuff that had been going on between her and Frank. I felt like a complete asshole.

"You misunderstood," I said quickly. "Of course I want you there. We always spend the Fourth of July together, right?"

I opened a third packet of Pop-Tarts, crumbled them into a cereal bowl, drowned them in milk, and offered them to Seattle. "Thanks," she said. "I haven't had real food in forever. Scott and I ate at this Indian place last night. It was . . . different."

She spooned some of the Pop-Tart mush into her mouth, looking up like she was testing me for a reaction. So I smiled and said, "Indian, huh?"

"Yeah. It was okay. Some of the stuff was really salty, though. Not in a good way, like the chili cheese fries you make, but pucker-your-mouth salty.

"He's building me a skateboard," she continued. "It's going to be totally rad." She pushed her bowl in my direction, and I dug into her leftover mush. "I had to borrow the money from Jesse," she confessed. "I was thinking I might try to get a job at the skate shop this fall."

I didn't tell her I already knew; no use in selling Jesse out like that. Instead, I said, "That's awesome, Sea. I bet you'd be good working there. You'd make sure those guys gave all the skater girls the respect they deserve."

She laughed, and her whole face lit up. "You know it."

It felt like the tension that had been growing

between us was starting to relax, and I didn't want to waste the opportunity. "So you're feeling okay?" I asked, trying to sound casual about it.

"What, you mean about last night?"

I nodded.

She shook her head like she used to when she still had dreads and liked to make them flop in her eyes. And then, as if she realized they were gone, she rubbed her fingers over her peach-fuzzed scalp. "He told me he wanted to know me again. Said that's why he came back. The stupid thing? I want to believe him. I hate that I want to believe him, but I do."

"What's wrong with that, though?"

She rolled her eyes. "Because you know—you *know*—it's not true. I mean, he probably *thinks* it is, but it'll be just like before he left for good. You know, when he'd disappear for a week or two, come back begging Layla to forgive him. The minute things get tough he'll be out of here again. Why do I want to put myself through that?"

"I don't know, Sea. Jesse said he looked really devastated last night. Maybe he's really changed this time."

"Maybe."

I opened the last pack of Pop-Tarts and offered one

to her, but she shook her head. As I started to nibble on mine, she said, "I think I missed this."

"What?"

"You and me. Talking. There hasn't been a lot of talking lately."

I had to agree with her. "I guess it was bound to happen. You know, when we really started dating."

Her right eyebrow shot up. "So you're *dating* her now?"

"Yeah. Why?"

"I thought she had a boyfriend."

I balled the foil wrapper and shot it into the trash can. "She did. Now she doesn't."

"That's convenient."

"What's that supposed to mean?"

"Nothing." She shrugged. "You can date whoever you want."

"Yeah, but why do you hate her so much? It's obvious, you know, how much you hate her."

"Sort of like how you hate Scott?"

"That's different."

"Why?" she demanded. "Because he's a skater? Because he's in college?"

"No," I said, even though both were partly true. "If

you want to know the real reason, it's because in less than two months, he's out of here. And I know how well you deal with goodbyes."

I meant it sincerely, but she must've misread something in my voice. "Go to hell," she spat, before running upstairs and slamming her bedroom door.

So much for talking.

Ghetto Blaster

With the freeze back on between me and Sea, I had a whole lotta time to kill, and absolutely nothing to do. I wanted to call Sarah, as she was the only good thing in my life right then, but I knew she was busy. Besides, I didn't want to scare her off. Better to wait for her to come to me.

After an unsuccessful attempt to find something watchable on TV, I spotted my SAT prep book sitting on the coffee table. The last place I'd seen it was the back of my closet, where I'd chucked it the week before. Layla must've gone looking for it. I had a feeling she wouldn't let up on me until I'd taken every single practice test twice.

I'd bombed the new SATs the previous spring—got a 440 on math and a whopping 360 on verbal. And don't get me started on the essay portion. Needless to say, I couldn't even get into Delaware with those scores. Layla took me to one of those test prep centers, but a single course would've cost hundreds of dollars—dollars we didn't have. So she bought me this book off the discount rack at Barnes & Noble instead.

The only thing I'd learned so far was why I sucked at standardized tests:

A) My memory was for shit, so forget about me knowing which math equation to use for each of the different problems.

B) Ditto for vocabulary.

C) There was usually more than one right answer to the reading questions, and for the life of me I couldn't figure out how one could be more right than another.

D) Staring at all the empty bubbles made me sleepy.

E) All of the above.

Disgusted, I shoved the book under the couch. When would Layla learn? I was never going to be like Jesse, or even Sea. The only reason her grades were so bad was that school bored the hell out of her. If they'd let her take classes like the Physics of Skateboarding, she'd be on the honor roll every marking period.

Upstairs I dug through my newly organized closet, trying to figure out what I should wear to the party the next day. In my mind I saw the cover of Rod Stewart's *A Night on the Town,* his classic album featuring "Tonight's the Night." On it, he was standing in what looked like an upper-crust backyard of sorts, sporting an ascot and holding a glass of champagne. There was this old-timey straw hat on his head, like someone in a barbershop quartet might wear, only cooler. You could just tell how hard the ladies must've been sweating Rod.

Luckily, I had a hat almost exactly like it. I'd found it during one of our trips around the local thrift store circuit. The only difference was that the band on mine was dark red, whereas Rod's was black.

It would be too hot to wear the long-sleeved white shirt and sports coat that completed Rod's outfit. But I did have a short-sleeved button-down that had superthin blue pinstripes on it, and I could raid Layla's closet for a scarf that could double as an ascot. Slap on some denim cutoffs and my blue Chucks, and I would be looking *fine.*

What to do, what to do? Jesse wouldn't be home

from work for another hour or so, and who knew if he'd even be talking to me? Then, a flash of inspiration. I'd make Sarah that mix tape. An old-school, all-Rod mix tape—the kind of tape that would not only introduce her to the true genius of Rod, but also let her know exactly how I felt.

I grabbed some paper and a pen and pulled all my Rod CDs off their shelf and onto the floor. Making this mix would require some serious planning. Not just the song selection, but also the order I should put them in. I drafted about seven different potential playlists before finally settling on the first. Then, just as I was finishing the first side, the tape ran out in the middle of "Last Summer" and I had to start all over again.

I was so absorbed in what I was certain would be my finest creation that I didn't hear Layla come into my room. It wasn't until she asked me to turn the music down that I realized she was there.

"I need to talk to you," she said, sitting on the edge of my bed.

"Before you start, I'm sorry about the car. I shouldn't have taken it."

"No, you shouldn't have, but that's not what I want to talk to you about."

"Oh?"

She looked at the mess of tapes and CDs forming a circle around me on the floor. "What's all this about?"

"Just this girl," I said. "She invited us all to this barbecue tomorrow, so I wanted to bring a thank-you gift."

"What makes you think you aren't grounded?"

"Am I?"

She sighed. "You should be."

"But I'm not, right?"

Another sigh. "Critter, I need you to listen for a minute, okay?"

I nodded.

"What happened yesterday made me realize that I am spending way too much time at work. I can't keep going like this. So on Monday, when you and Sea start summer school, I'm going to take a two-week leave of absence, to figure some things out."

"Things? What things?"

"Like how I can cut back my hours and still get the bills paid on time."

"What you need to do," I said, "is get Frank to cough up some cash. I mean, Jesus, you've been raising his daughter longer than he ever did."

"I won't do that," she said stiffly.

"Why not?"

"Because I won't. End of discussion."

I sighed. "Your problem is you're too damned proud. It's not weak to ask Frank for money—it's practical."

"Practical?" she repeated. "*You're* lecturing me on practical? Wouldn't it have been *practical* for you to spend the past few weeks studying, instead of chasing some girl and working on your tan?"

"At least that *girl* understands why school's not my thing," I said coldly.

"Oh? And why is that exactly? Because Shakespeare's not as 'cool' as Rod Stewart?"

"No!" I exploded. "It's because it's too damned *hard*!"

Her face softened. I had to look away.

"I know school doesn't come as easy to you as it does to Jesse," she said. "But that doesn't mean you shouldn't try."

"I've *been* trying," I shot back.

"Then why didn't you sign up for the free tutoring? Or join that study group Jesse told you about?"

"It wouldn't help," I said. "Let's just face it: I'm stupid, okay? *End of discussion.*"

"You are *not* stupid. You're just . . . easily frustrated."

"Christ!" I yelled. "What is it with you and school?

Let me get a job, make some money. At least then I'd be useful."

"I can't say I haven't thought about you working part-time. But, Boo, if you don't get those grades up, you're not going to college. Do you want to be forty and working at a Wendy's? *I* certainly don't want that for you."

"Has it ever occurred to you that maybe that's all I'm cut out for?"

She shook her head. "I don't buy that, not for a second."

I didn't want to be having this conversation. Not about school, not about my future, and definitely not about my mother's debt. Especially not since the bulk of it came from Frank. Why should I have to pay for her poor taste in men?

"What do you want from me?" I asked her. "You won't let me work, and I don't see how me getting Bs is going to help you put food on the table."

"That isn't your problem."

"If it's not my problem," I snapped, "then why are we even having this conversation?"

Layla seemed surprised by the sharpness of my tone. She opened her mouth like she was going to say something, closed it, then opened and closed it again. Finally, she said, "Forget I said a word."

Jesse would've followed her out. *He* would've given her a hug, apologized for being such a shit, and listened to whatever it was she had to say. I had a feeling that was all she was looking for. But I wasn't Jesse.

I locked my door, cranked up the volume on my stereo, and went back to making Sarah's mix.

You Wear It Well

I suffered the rest of the day in silence. It seemed that in the past twenty-four hours, I'd managed to piss off every single person in my family, and no one was talking to me. I even placed a last-ditch call to Sarah, hoping for a little human contact, but I got her voice mail and she never called me back.

Around midnight, Jesse knocked on my door and asked me what time we had to leave for the party the next day.

"How do you know about the party?"

"Sea told me. What, am I not invited?"

"It's not that," I said. "It's just . . ."

"What? Spit it out."

"I didn't think you'd want to go."

"Look," he said. "I was pissed. I'm still a little pissed. But I've got the day off and the three of us always hang out on the Fourth. So, yeah—I'm going."

"Which means Sea is going, too."

He nodded. "Don't forget Scott."

"Of course not," I said tightly. "Who could forget about him?"

●

The party was starting at two, so I figured if we left at two-thirty, we'd get there forty-five minutes into the festivities—just the right side of fashionably late.

I was ready with time to spare. To keep busy, I put away all the CDs and tapes I'd dragged out to make Sarah's mix. I even made my bed; that was how bored I was. When Jesse wandered in, I was working on the last hospital corner.

"Hey," I said. "What do you think of my outfit? Slick, right?"

He snorted. "You're acting like a girl."

"I'm not," I protested. "I just . . . you know. Want to impress her."

"Sorry, bro, but I don't think you're going to do it with your keen fashion sense."

"Bite me."

"Oh, all right," he said with an annoyed sigh. "You might want to lose the scarf, but the rest of it looks okay."

"Thanks." I smiled. "Wait until you see her, Jess. Hear her voice. She's like . . . I don't even *know* what she's like! Delicious—that's the word. *Delicious.*"

"Apples are delicious," he said. "Girls are just girls."

I shook my head. "You wait. Someday you'll meet some obsessive-compulsive neat freak who shares your love of early-nineties hip-hop and it'll be all over. Mark my words, man. Mark my words."

"I love how you think you're some expert on the subject."

"More like a *sex*pert."

"Whatever," Jesse said, grinning. "But remember: just 'cause you've made your bed doesn't mean you'll get laid in it."

"Ha-ha." I fluffed my pillow and set it down. "Hey . . . why aren't you dressed?"

" 'Cause I'm getting in the shower?"

"*Now?*" I fumed. "Now you are getting in the shower?"

He rolled his eyes. "Calm down. It's only two o'clock."

"No it's not! It's almost two-thirty!"

"I'm not the one you should be worried about," Jesse said. "Sea left like three hours ago, and I haven't seen her since."

"Well, that's just *perfect*," I snarled as he ducked into the bathroom. The lock clicked behind him. "Ten minutes!" I yelled through the door. "Ten minutes and I'm leaving your sorry asses behind!"

I stomped back downstairs and collapsed on the couch. Where was she? Hanging with Skater Boy, obviously. I couldn't stop thinking about what would happen next—what kind of humiliation Sea and her new boyfriend might be cooking up for me. I also couldn't stop sweating. The back of my neck was so moist it took two paper towels to mop up.

It was going on three o'clock when I heard the front door slam. I was beyond pissed and was ready to tell my sister this when Skater Boy came into view. He was wearing baggy army pants, a skintight tank top, and black leather shit-kicker boots pulled up over the cuffs of his pants.

"Who the hell are you supposed to be?" I asked. "Rambo?"

"You're one to talk," he shot back. "Gatsby."

"Gat-who?"

"Gatsby. Jay Gatsby? From *The Great Gatsby*?"

"Yeah, whatever, dude. What's your name again? Cooter?"

He smiled, a patient little smile that made me want to pop him one. "Scooter," he said. "But most people call me Scott."

"So where's my sister?"

"Right here," Seattle replied, wandering in from the kitchen. "Is that what you're wearing?"

I took one look at her and almost died. It was my worst fear realized. The right half of her peach-fuzzed scalp had been dyed with stripes of red, so that next to the white-blond tufts tipped in blue they made her head look like the American flag. And it didn't stop there. She'd put on a matching red tube top that made her boobs look like they could fall out at any second. She'd paired this with a bright blue cheerleading skirt worn over her jeans, which she'd cuffed about three inches at the bottom. And, what else? A pair of boots that looked remarkably like the ones Skater Boy had strapped on his feet. He put his arm around her protectively.

"You," I said, because I didn't know what else to say.

"Me what?" she asked.

I shook my head. "Nothing."

Jesse came bounding down the stairs then, and all three of us turned to see what sort of costume he'd put on. Thankfully, he was wearing crisp khaki shorts, a fitted navy blue polo shirt, and a pair of loafers. When he hit the bottom step, he took one look at us and burst out laughing.

"Shut up," I said. "And get in the car."

"Don't worry, bro," he said after the laugh had died down to a chuckle. "I'm sure your girlfriend will appreciate the arrival of the freak brigade."

Having a Party

Sarah's street was so jam-packed with parked SUVs that I had to swing around the corner just to find a spot. It wasn't any hotter than usual, but the back of my hair was soaked in sweat, which I could feel trickling down my neck.

"It's the hat," Jesse said as I was wiping away some of the wetness. "Traps the heat on your head."

I ignored him and started walking toward Sarah's house, which I hadn't counted on being quite so big. It looked three stories tall, faced in real brick and white wood siding, with a choke chain of hedges so perfectly trimmed that Edward Scissorhands himself could have been their gardener.

If Sea hadn't brought Skater Boy, I might've stopped there. I could've said something like, "This scene looks whack. Let's bolt and go to the Riverfront instead." But Skater Boy would know I was wussing out, and I wasn't about to lose face in front of him.

So I kept walking around to the back, where all the noise was coming from.

There were people covering every square inch of green. Women in lawn chairs, drinking out of plastic cups that had paper umbrellas stuck in them. Girls in the pool, riding the shoulders of guys in what looked like a match of water chicken. Men standing around in a circle topped by a cloud of smoke, watching, I guessed, the pig get charbroiled.

The four of us stood there, right inside the gate. This wasn't like any party I'd ever been to. Most of our parties were held in basements, the Sex Pistols cranked, couples making out in dark corners, people passing beers and cigarettes and the occasional joint. Not this outdoorsy thing, with a white tent shading part of the yard, covering a long row of tables and benches that were set like it was the Last Supper and not some Fourth of July barbecue.

I was the first to spy the huge metal buckets, filled with ice and water, beer bottlenecks peeking out the tops. I made a beeline for them, grabbed a Bud, twisted off the cap, and downed three-quarters of it in one long gulp. It was too much too quick, and the minute after I swallowed, I let out this belch that was so loud, it embarrassed even me. Some dudes in shorts and black kneesocks turned to see the source of the noise, so I grinned and waved and tried to pretend like everything was cool.

Seattle brushed by me to grab a beer of her own, muttering, "So much for the dry party."

I didn't take the bait, deciding my energy was better spent trying to locate Sarah in a sea of golf dads and silky-blond soccer moms. All the kids, I guessed, were either in the pool or near it. I focused my attention there, and sure enough, not thirty seconds later I saw Sarah pulling herself out using the ladder. She was showing more of her skin than I'd ever seen—in real life, anyway—and man, it was a sight to behold, her tanned and toned bod against a white bikini top and flag-patterned swim shorts.

I swatted Jess on the arm and pointed my chin toward Sarah. "That's her," I said.

"Dude," he said.

"Yeah," I said.

"*Dude,*" he said again.

"I told you," I said. "You get it now?"

He nodded without saying another word.

Sarah greeted me with a quick hug, her wet bikini top barely making contact before she pulled away. It didn't stop me from popping an instant boner, which would have been tragic had I been the kind of person who didn't wear shorts two sizes too big.

The spirit of Rod was surely watching over me.

Sarah turned to Jesse and introduced herself to him. As they shook hands she said, "I've heard a lot about you."

"I've heard a lot about you, too," he said, grinning. "A *lot.* All good, though, so no worries."

"Really?" Sarah said. She was smiling, but it was the kind of smile you wear to mask something else. Jesse's gushing had probably thrown her off a bit.

Before I could get her away from him, Sarah excused herself to say hello to more guests. She didn't indicate whether I should follow her, so I hesitated. The pause gave me time to hear Sea trying to bum a smoke off one of the nearby golf dads. He was holding a small plate of deviled eggs and there was a pack of Marlboro reds poking out the top pocket of his patriotic-plaid shirt.

"Aren't you a little too young to be smoking?" he asked, not unkindly.

"Aren't you a little too fat to be eating those?" she shot back.

As if on automatic pilot, I grabbed Sea's arm and started dragging her back toward the gate, throwing an "excuse us" over my shoulder almost as an afterthought.

"Get off me," she growled, trying to shake free.

I dug into her arm even harder. "What is your problem?"

"Let go!"

"I will not let you start any trouble here, you got me? So you'd better behave."

"Or what?" she snarled.

"Listen," I said, starting to twist her arm a bit. "I

don't know why you hate that girl so much. But you know what? I like her. I like her *a lot.* And you know what else? She likes me, too. And I'm probably going to sleep with her later tonight, because her goddamned boyfriend was too stupid to leave his jock friends and play escort at this party.

"So if you do anything—anything at all—to screw this up for me . . . I will make you pay."

"Ooh, I'm so scared."

"Good," I said. "You should be."

I threw her arm down and walked away.

seattle

Bruised

My first instinct was to grab Scott and get the hell out. But my pride was way stronger than Critter's grip, and I knew if I slinked away, he would win. It was all about power, and who had it. If I stayed, I might be able to wrestle some of it back.

So I picked my chin up off my boobs, as Layla liked to say, and marched forward. Scott started walking toward me, this concerned Boy Scout look on his face. "What was that all about?" he asked. "Did he hurt you?"

Before I could answer, Jesse grabbed my non-bruised arm and I was dragged away for the second time in five minutes.

"Why are you doing this?" he asked.

"Me? What am *I* doing? Did you see him assault me?"

Jesse snorted. "Stop antagonizing him. He's only giving you a hard time because you've been so moody lately."

I pulled away from him. "Thanks a lot."

"Come on, Sea. Let's get real, okay? You're acting weird. You have been ever since you guys went to that pool the first time."

I folded my arms across my chest. "Yeah, and . . . ?"

"I don't know. Maybe I'm imagining things. But . . . did something happen between you and Critter?"

"What do you mean by 'happen'? We're fighting, that's what happened."

"Yeah, I know," he said. "It's just . . . you guys have been acting really off. Like, jealous and possessive of each other. More like—"

"Like what?" I demanded.

Jesse sighed. "Never mind."

I stomped back over to Scott, so pissed off that I could actually *feel* the scowl stamped on my face.

"Seattle," he said. Just my name, nothing else—but his voice was so tender. If I had been a weaker person, it might have made me break.

"What?" I snapped.

"What's going on?"

"Nothing's going on!" I said. "I'm just hungry. Jesus. Aren't you hungry?"

He didn't answer me; he only kept giving me that concerned look of his.

"Well, *I* am," I said. "I'm famished."

He didn't look completely convinced, but he definitely seemed less concerned. "Okay, let's get some food."

There were all these food stations scattered across the yard. One for finger food, another for lemonade and punch, and another that was a full-on bar, surrounded by these giant tubs of beers. It was like something you'd see in a magazine. Plus, there were flags *everywhere.* Fabric flags, plastic flags, flags pinned on a circus tent they had set up in one corner like a mess hall. And there were *Survivor* tiki torches planted throughout, each one gussied up with a stars-and-stripes ribbon bow. There were even these totally tacky flag-patterned pinwheels marking a path toward the circus tent/mess hall. Not to mention the people. Almost all of them had on those flag T-shirts that Old Navy and the Gap hawked each year. Literally flags as far as the eye could see.

When we reached the finger food station, Scott said, "Oh, excellent—they have crudités."

"Crew-da-what?"

"Crudités," he repeated, smiling. Then he leaned in, like he was about to share a state secret, and stage-whispered, "It's a fancy word for raw vegetables." He grabbed a baby carrot, chomped down on it, and gave me a wink.

We filled our flag plates with more crudités, some of those deviled eggs I saw the fat guy eating earlier, and fruit kabobs. Then we walked over to a willow tree in the far back corner of the yard and took a seat under it. Scott swirled a piece of cauliflower into some green dip he'd spooned on his plate, and I watched his mouth as he ate it.

"Do you want to try some?" he asked.

"Sure."

He dunked a fresh piece of cauliflower into the green goop and held it up to my mouth. It surprised me, him trying to feed me, so at first I didn't do anything; I just sat there like some kind of idiot.

"Go on," he said. "It's pretty good."

I took the chunk and my lips brushed his fingers. Hot sparks flowed throughout my entire bod. Somehow cauliflower dipped in green goop had just become about the sexiest thing going. I swallowed hard.

"Are we ever gonna do it?" I blurted out.

"Do what?"

"You know," I said. "*It.*"

"Oh," Scott said. "I don't know, are we?"

"You tell me."

His eyebrows bunched up some, like he was deep in thought, and he set his plate aside. "You know," he said after a while. "This is the second time you've propositioned me for sex."

"And it's the second time you've acted like you don't want to sleep with me."

"Seattle," he said, in the meat-tenderizer voice. "Of course I want to sleep with you."

"So what's the problem?"

Scott sighed. "I don't think it's the right time."

"I didn't know there could be a wrong time for boys," I said, folding my arms across my chest. "Maybe it's more like I'm the wrong *person.*"

"No," he said. "That's not it at all."

I looked away. "Whatever."

Scott's lips brushed my shoulder, giving me goose-flesh all over. He leaned into my ear real close and said softly, "Will you at least let me explain?" I nodded, and when his right hand crawled over to my left one, I let him lace his fingers through mine.

"I didn't want to tell you until after the party," he began, "but I got this message when I was out with you the other day. The thing is there's a really good possibility that I'll have to go home sooner than I thought."

Katja.

He was still talking, but I'd already tuned him out. I should've known this would happen. When I first met Scott I thought we'd hook up a couple of times and then he'd fly back to Washington and that would be the end of it. After the other day, though . . . I'd fooled myself into thinking he might really like me—that maybe this thing had long-term potential. He wasn't my boyfriend, but it was the closest I'd ever come to feeling like someone's girlfriend. Too bad I was only a place-holder, until his real girlfriend came to claim him.

". . . and it's a really great opportunity," he continued. "I'd be a manager for Treasures of Trash, which is a program offshoot of Habitat for Humanity. Basically

I'd be going through donated building materials and seeing what can be salvaged for—"

"You should've told me you still loved her," I interrupted.

"What? Who?"

"Isn't that really why you're going back?" I asked. "For Katja."

He shook his head. "Katja's in Austin, but even if she wasn't—"

And that's when it happened. Sarah was standing by the lemonade, pouring herself a glass, when I saw a tall dark-haired guy come up from behind, throw his arms around her waist, and hug her so tightly her feet came up off the ground. Then he turned her around and started kissing her—really kissing her—with his hands pressed against her starred-and-striped butt cheeks.

I knew in a heartbeat that it was her boyfriend, the one Critter thought she'd gotten rid of. Scott was saying something about the job when I jumped up so fast I knocked him in the nose.

"Sorry," I said. "I've got to go."

I had to find Critter before he found her.

The backyard was big but not enormous, so it

shouldn't have been too hard to locate him. Especially since he was wearing that ridiculous hat. The problem was that there were way too many people crammed into the space, and everyone was wearing the same damned colors, so no one person really stood out.

I closed the lid on a cooler and climbed on top, craning my neck until I found him. He was loading up a plate at the finger food station, which wasn't so very far from the lemonade station, where Sarah and her boyfriend were mauling each other. I leapt off the cooler and was jogging over to Critter when he turned and saw them. I knew he did, because he got that deer-in-headlights look on his face. Then he set his plate down, but he put it too far over the table's edge and it fell onto the grass. He didn't even notice.

He started walking toward them, and I thought about intervening but had a feeling it would make things worse. So I hung back a little, close enough to hear what they were saying, but not so close that Critter knew I was there.

"Sarah," he said.

She ducked away from her boyfriend, wiped the corner of her mouth with the side of her hand, and giggled. "Oh, hi, Critter. This—this is Duncan Mackenzie."

Duncan gave a little wave and said, "Don't I know you?"

"He goes to Haley," Sarah explained. "I met his sister while guarding at the pool and the three of us hung out a bit."

Critter didn't say another word; he just stared at her. "Nice to meet you," Duncan said, but he was looking off into the distance. He must've spotted someone he knew, because he shouted out a "yo," tapped Sarah on the arm, and said, "Looks like Andy Rockwell brought his new girlfriend. We should go say hi and check her out."

She nodded, and as Duncan led her away, she turned to face my brother and mouthed a silent apology. But if she felt bad, she didn't let it faze her, because less than a minute later she was hugging that Andy guy and squealing like a little girl.

Critter still hadn't moved. I went up to him and touched his arm. "Hey," I said.

"What do you know?" He blinked a few times and took off his hat. "Guess I won't be getting any after all."

I knew him well enough to know that right this second sex was the furthest thing from his mind. He'd meant what he'd said before about really liking her.

"I'm sorry," I said.

"No you're not."

"I am," I said. "It was a shitty thing for her to do."

He didn't disagree. "Go get your boyfriend. Jess, too. I'll meet you in the car." He took what looked like a cassette tape from his pocket, dropped it on the ground, and smashed it with his foot as he walked away.

Just like that, the party was over.

My Kingdom for a Kiss

No one said anything on the drive home. It was so dark and quiet in the car that I felt like we were leaving someone's funeral instead of what was supposed to be a fun summer barbecue.

At the house, I tried to send Scott on his way, but he insisted we talk.

"What's there to talk about?" I asked. "My summer class starts tomorrow, so it's not like we'd have spent that much time together anyway."

"That's not true, and you know it." He reached for my hand but I jerked away.

"Seriously?" I said. "You should go."

"But—"

"I'm fine. Right now I need to take care of my brother."

Inside, Jesse was making a grilled cheese sandwich. "I didn't get to eat," he explained. "You want one?"

"No thanks."

"So," he said, "I guess you were right about the pool bunny, huh?"

Oddly enough, I didn't care about being right. All I kept seeing was that hurt expression on Critter's face— the one that looked exactly how I felt. "I'm going to go talk to him."

Jesse winced. "You think that's a good idea right now?"

"Yeah," I said. "I do."

As I headed upstairs, I could hear one of Critter's favorite Rod Stewart songs—"Broken Arrow." A syrupy ballad at best, but once he'd told me that he didn't mind the cheese, because the song sounded like what he thought love must feel like.

I knocked on the door.

"Go away," he yelled.

He had the song on repeat; I let it play through two more times before knocking again.

"I said go away!"

"I'm not going anywhere," I said. "So open the door."

He swore some, but eventually the lock clicked and the door swung open. Critter flopped back onto his bed. The clothes he'd worn to Sarah's party were in a heap on the floor, except for his cutoffs, which he still had on.

I sat on the edge of the bed. "I really am sorry, Critter."

"Whatever."

"That's my line," I joked. He didn't respond. "Do you want to talk about it?"

"Nope."

"I know things have been weird the past couple of weeks," I said, "but we used to talk about everything. I want you to know you still can."

"No, I can't." He sat up, scooted off the end of the bed, and popped out the CD. "Things are different now."

"Different how?"

"You know."

And I guessed I *did* know, but I didn't want to. I didn't like the way things were turning out. I wanted it to be like it was before.

Critter plopped down to the floor in front of his

bed, his back leaning against the mattress. He started flipping through a small stack of CDs, got disgusted, and pushed them away. I slid off the bed until I was sitting next to him. "I wish we'd never gone to that stupid pool."

"Yeah?" he said. "Me too."

Critter's face was sort of crumpled up, like maybe he was going to start crying, and a strong, clear pain shot through my chest. I didn't want to see him like this. Sad, and so small, like he was that kid I first met in Pappy's Pizzeria all those years ago.

I bent down, slowly, over his bare shoulder, touching my lips to his hot skin. Lingering afterward, breathing on the spot I'd just marked with my mouth. Then I heard his sharp intake of breath and pulled away. Critter scrambled up off the floor and said, "Get out."

"What? Why?"

He pulled on a T-shirt and shoved his feet into the sneakers he'd been wearing earlier. "Fine," he said. "I'll leave."

"Where are you going?" I called after him, but he didn't answer; he kept walking.

It was just one kiss, but I had a feeling it had changed everything.

critter

I Could Feel the Whole World
Turn Around Underneath Me

I walked away from that house as fast as my feet could take me. I wasn't sure what that kiss had been about, and I didn't want to stick around and find out. The minute her mouth had connected with my shoulder, the only—and I mean *only*—thing I could think about was the shower incident.

Why couldn't I erase it from my brain?

I half walked, half ran to the Movie King, so that by the time I arrived I was fairly hot and sweaty. I said a silent prayer of thanks when I saw Shelli standing behind the register. Without saying a word, I took her hand and led her into the back room, where I slammed her up against a shelf of videos, sending more than a few brown plastic cases crashing to the floor.

Shelli didn't seem to mind.

"I've missed you," I whispered.

She sighed softly. "Me too."

We were still kissing and groping when she stretched out her arm to turn the lock on the door. Then she shook out her bright red hair—bottle red, not natural—and slid down to her knees. I wound my fingers through her hair, almost petting her while pressing her slightly closer. It was a move that always, always elicited noises from Shelli's busy mouth, and in a few minutes, I was done.

As I pulled up my pants, I reached for a tissue from the desk and handed it to Shelli. "Thanks," she said, sitting back on her feet, still on the floor.

"No," I said. "Thank *you.*"

I reached for the door.

"That's *it*?" Shelli asked. "You're leaving? Just like that?"

"Sorry," I said. "Did you want something else?"

I made the mistake of looking into her eyes as I said this. Otherwise, I wouldn't have seen the first tears fall.

"Screw you," she said with a sniffle.

"Shelli," I said, placing my hand on her shoulder.

She shook it off violently. "Don't you say my name *now*."

She was crying harder, really wailing, and I didn't know how to make her stop. I felt like a total shit, but as I replayed what had just happened it didn't seem any different from the other times we'd hooked up. When had the rules changed?

"Look," I said. "I never promised to be your boyfriend or anything."

It sounded way nastier than I had intended, and I'm sure my face registered shock even before Shelli hauled off and punched me in the groin. I hit the floor with a thunk as Shelli grabbed the shelf and lifted herself up.

"Get out of my store," she said, her hands shaking by her sides. "And don't you ever—*ever*—come back here again."

Farewell

I'd reached a new low.

From the Movie King I limped across the street to the gas station, looking for a pay phone. It was broken, so I had to cross two lanes of busy traffic just to get to Community Plaza, which, as it turned out, didn't even *have* any pay phones. I let out a howl, spotted one of those metal newspaper dispenser things, and kicked it as hard as I could.

"You're gonna break your foot if you're not careful."

I whirled around to find Frank standing behind me. "What the hell are you doing here?"

"Getting smokes." He held up a pack of Parliaments. "Want one?"

"No."

Frank shook out a cigarette, struck a match, and inhaled deeply. "I owe you an apology," he said, not looking at me.

"What for?"

"Do I have to say it?"

There were so many things he could be apologizing for, I couldn't figure out which screwup this apology was meant for. Regardless, I was the last person he needed to be apologizing to.

"Why are you telling me this?"

"Because my daughter won't talk to me," he said.

"Can you blame her?"

He chuckled. "No, I guess not."

It was uncomfortable, standing there with him, his words hanging in the air like the smoke from his cigarette. Finally Frank said, "You'll be glad to know I'm going back to Scranton."

"What? When?"

"Tonight."

"Does Sea know? Layla?" I took his silence as confirmation that they didn't. "You have to tell them," I said. "It'd be really shitty of you not to."

Frank laughed, low and bitter. "No one's gonna miss me, kid. You said it yourself—you were all better off with me gone."

"That's a coward's response."

"Is it?" Frank took one last drag off his cigarette, dropped it on the concrete, and stomped it out. "Fine, then. I guess I'm a coward." He reached around to his back pocket and took out an envelope. "I was going to drop this off at the house, but you can take it for me, can't you?"

"What is it?"

"What's it look like? A letter."

I eyed the envelope, which looked too fat to be just a letter. "How much cash you got in there?"

"Enough."

He handed it to me. "I still think you should at least say goodbye."

"You do it for me," he said.

I started to walk away when Frank called to me. "Hey," he said. "I left the number of the place where I'll be staying. Make sure Seattle gets it. Tell her, you know, to give me a call. When she's ready."

He climbed into his Olds before I could tell him I would.

Some Guys Have All the Luck

I walked back home but didn't go inside. Thankfully, the keys to the Cougar were still in my pocket, so I fired up the beast and headed to Christiana Hospital. It was time for a little coffee talk with my mom.

Layla looked surprised to see me. "What happened to your party?"

"Oh, that," I said, waving her off. "Nothing. Listen, can you take a break?"

She eyed me suspiciously. "Sure," she said. "Give me a few."

Fifteen minutes later we were sitting across from each other at a small table in the cafeteria. She blew on her too-hot coffee while I retrieved the fat envelope Frank had given me and slid it across the table.

"What's this?" she asked.

"Open it."

A bunch of bills spilled out onto the table. Hundreds, twenties, tens. A note scrawled on a piece of motel stationery dropped on top of the pile.

"What's it say, Mom?"

"His horse hit."

"What?"

Layla shook her head. "Frank. He's playing the horses again. Went down to Atlantic City mid-May and hit on a horse. According to this," she continued, tapping the letter, "he's been living off the winnings ever since."

"So much for changing."

We sorted the bills into piles and Layla did a quick count. "Jesus," she said, her voice a near whisper.

"What?"

"There's eight thousand dollars here."

"Holy shit!"

We were silent for a minute, both of us staring at the wad of money resting between us. Eight thousand dollars could pay for a lot of things. Fixing our central air-conditioning, for one. A new muffler for the Cougar, for another.

Layla opened her mouth to speak but I cut her off. "No," I said. "You're not giving it back. How much of your savings did he piss away at the track? He *owes* you this money."

Her face clouded over and she shoved the cash back into its envelope. "We'll talk about this later," she said. "Right now I'm going to see if I can find anyone to cover the rest of my shift."

Another fifteen minutes and we were heading home. Layla was staring out the window, a dark look on her face. "I don't know how I'm going to tell Missy."

"You don't have to," I said. "I'll do it for you."

"But it's my fault. I'm the one who pushed Frank on her again. I really thought—"

"You weren't wrong," I cut in. "He left Sea his address and phone number, didn't he? It's a start."

She patted my knee. "You take good care of your old mom, don't you?"

"Sometimes."

"No," Layla said. "Most times." She leaned forward and turned the eight-track off. "I've been thinking about our conversation the other night—what you said about school."

"*Mom!*" I said. "I seriously cannot talk about this right now."

"So don't talk—*listen.*"

I gritted my teeth, waiting for her to deliver her seven hundredth lecture of the summer on Why Critter Needs to Be a Better Student.

"You remember Trish, right? The cute blond nurse you had the crush on? She went to Haley, too—graduated five or six years ago. Anyway, she was telling me that she did this work release program her senior year. Took three classes in the morning and then worked at the hospital in the afternoons for credit."

"And . . . ?"

"And I was thinking maybe you could do something like that. You'd have to pass your summer class, of course, and get Cs or better next year to stay in the program. But I've been thinking that maybe you would learn better outside the classroom than in one."

I couldn't believe what I was hearing. For as long as I could remember, Layla had been saying stuff like "If only you'd try harder . . ." and "I wish you'd really apply yourself." Now this?

"So what's the catch?" I said. "There is a catch, right?"

"I want you in tutoring. Effective immediately."

I pulled into the driveway and put the car in park. "That's it? *That's* the catch?"

She nodded. "I'm not giving up on the idea of you going to college, either."

"Where would I work? I mean, I don't even know what I want to do with my life."

"That's the best part," she said, smiling. "Trish's boyfriend, Randy, works at WJBR. They're looking for an intern for fall and she thinks he could get you in. You're supposed to call him tomorrow when you get home from school—if you're interested, that is."

Interested? The thought of me interning at an adult contemporary radio station—a very Rod-friendly kind of place—*and* only having to do half days at Haley was almost enough to erase the ugliness I'd been dealing with all day.

Almost.

"We should go in," Layla said. "We can talk more about this later."

We found Sea and Jesse sitting in the middle of the living room floor, playing rummy.

"Jess," Layla said, "can you excuse us for a minute?"

"This is about Frank, isn't it?" Sea asked.

Layla nodded. "How did you know?"

"Why else would you come home in the middle of a shift?" She leaned back against the couch. "Jesse can stay."

The four of us sat on the carpet together. Layla took the envelope out of her purse and handed it to Seattle. "Frank gave this to you?" she asked.

"Yes," Layla said. "And I'm giving it to you. For college."

Seattle rolled her eyes. "Screw that," she said. "Let's get the goddamned air-conditioning fixed already."

Layla started to protest but I jumped in. "There's more, Sea," I said. "Frank's gone."

"Gone?" she repeated. "Like dead gone?"

"No," I said. "Like back-to-Scranton gone."

"Oh." She sucked in a big breath and let it out slowly. *"Oh,"* she said again, more softly this time.

Layla reached out and stroked Sea's shoulder. "You okay, Missy?"

"Sure," she said, shrugging. "Why wouldn't I be?"

"You don't have to hide your disappointment," Layla said. "We can talk about it."

Sea pushed her hand away. "You don't get it. *I don't care.*"

"Of course you care."

"No!" she yelled. "*You* care. *I* never wanted him to come back to begin with."

"Lower your voice," Layla said. "Let's talk about this in a civilized tone."

"But I don't want to talk about it," Sea said. "I never want to talk about it again."

She got up and headed outside, slamming the door behind her. Layla nudged me. "Go after her, Boo. Make sure she's okay."

Outside, Sea was sitting on the front stoop. I sat down next to her and said, "So you really don't care, huh?"

She shook her head, but I read something different on her face. I put my arms around her. She was stiff at first, but then melted into my hug.

"You were right about Scott, you know," she said after a while. "He's leaving, too."

I frowned. "What do you mean?"

"He says he's got some mondo job waiting for him back home, but I doubt it."

"Why's that?"

She shrugged. "I don't really want to talk about it."

"Then why did you bring it up?"

She pulled away from me then, and I could see the tears clouding her eyes. I don't think I'd ever seen her look so beautiful.

"Sea?" I asked. "Why did you do that earlier?"

"Do what?"

"You know," I said quietly. "My shoulder."

"Oh, that." She sighed. "I don't know."

Seattle looked away, but I couldn't stop staring at her. Without even thinking about it, I reached for her chin and turned her face toward me.

"What are you doing?" she asked, but didn't jerk away. I cupped her face in my hands and leaned toward her, feeling her breath growing hotter on my face until our lips were touching. My heart beat wildly in my chest. The whole time I kept thinking, *What am I doing?* All I knew was that it felt right.

Sea pulled away from me so abruptly that I banged my head against her ear. "You shouldn't have done that."

My mouth was hanging open so far I must've looked like a goldfish out of his bowl. I watched as her hands flew to the top of her head, feeling for the dreadlocks I'd lopped off what seemed like for-ever ago.

"You're just feeling bad because of Sarah," she said, not looking at me. "That's all it is."

"No," I said. "It's not."

It was all so confusing. Sarah, Shelli, Sea. Especially Sea. I wondered if things would've been different if Layla hadn't hooked up with Frank. What if Sea and I had met on our own? Would we still have been friends? And if we had, would I still have felt so confused?

"It *is* because of Sarah," Sea said firmly. "It has to be."

"Maybe," I said, because I knew it was what she wanted to hear. "Maybe it is because of her."

A shaky smile spread across Sea's face. "It's going to be okay," she said. "For both of us." She patted my knee, stood up, and went back inside.

seattle

The Goodbye Boy

Layla left for the night shift around nine-thirty; twenty minutes later, the doorbell rang. *Scott.*

"I've got something for you." He handed me one of those huge Bloomingdale's bags with the twine handles. Inside were not one but two skateboards. The first was my old Kryptonics, with fresh grip tape on top and a set of brand-new wheels on the bottom. "For backup," Scott said.

The second was the one he'd built me. It was gorgeous. He'd coated the deck with shiny black paint. On the underside of the tail, he'd screened a cartoon outline of a girl's face. Her mouth was a cherry red heart and she had electric blue dreadlocks sprouting out of her head.

I could barely breathe. "She's beautiful!" I said when I found my voice.

"Yeah, she is," Scott said—but he wasn't looking at the board.

"I don't even know how to thank you."

He smiled. "Your face just did."

We stood there, me on one side of the door and him on the other. "Can I come in?" he asked in a tentative voice.

"Oh, right," I said. "Sure."

I held the new skateboard across my chest like a shield. Scott gestured to it and said, "You shouldn't ride it for another day or so. The lacquer needs time to set fully."

I nodded, still clutching it to me. "So when do you leave?"

"Tomorrow night," he said. "I'm taking the red-eye back home."

So that was it. He was really going, and I was really never going to see him again.

"I told my parents about you."

"Oh," I said, surprised. "Why?"

"Because they couldn't understand why I almost turned the job down."

This was . . . unexpected. Was it possible there really was some awesome job he simply couldn't pass up?

"What changed your mind?" I asked.

"They told me if I came back early, they'd pay for me to fly out here over winter break."

It took a minute for the words to sink in. "So you *are* coming back?"

"If you still want me to," he said slowly. "Then again, it *is* six months from now."

"Right," I said. "Maybe you'll have a girlfriend by then."

He shook his head. "I like you so much, Seattle. You have no idea how much I like you."

His words made me blush, and I couldn't hide the smile. "I like you, too," I confessed.

"I want to know you better. I want us to write, and talk on the phone, and I definitely want to see you again."

My smile turned into a nervous grin. "Me too," I said. "But what if—"

"Things change?" he finished for me. "Then we'll be honest with each other. I don't want to turn out to be another person who disappoints you. You don't deserve that."

He was saying all the right things in all the right ways, and yet something was still wrong. Maybe it was me. Maybe *I* was what was wrong.

Scott squeezed my hand. "Can I see you tomorrow after class? We never did get to log any skate time."

I shook my head. "This is hard enough as it is."

"Yeah," he said, nodding. "I know. Didn't hurt to ask, right?"

I walked him to the door. He leaned in for a good-bye kiss, but at the last second I turned my head, and his lips landed on my cheek. He looked startled and maybe a little hurt. "I'm sorry," I whispered.

"It's okay," he said. "I understand."

He hopped off the front stoop and gave a little wave. I stood there, watching him walk away, feeling like someone had ripped my heart right out of my chest. He was halfway down the street when he turned and hollered, "I *will* see you again. I can *feel* it!" He let out a whoop and thumped his chest like Tarzan. It made me laugh.

I closed the door and turned around. Critter was standing about six inches away and I yelped. "Jesus, you scared me!"

"Sorry," he said. "I just wanted to see if you were all right. I heard yelling."

"I'm fine."

"Yeah?"

"Yeah."

"Good," he said. "Now you can help me get ready for school."

Stoopid, Part II

"Are you sure about this?" I asked.

"Go on," he urged. "*Do it.*"

Critter thrust the shaver into my hand—the same one he'd used on me the week before.

"But you love this hair," I said.

"Correction—*used* to love it. Now I just want a change. Okay?"

I flicked the shaver on and felt it vibrate in my hand. "Can I at least close my eyes?"

"No!" he said. "Come on, Sea. It's no big deal, right? It'll grow back."

Fifteen minutes later I buzzed off the last bits of his bleached blond hair. Now Critter looked more like a marine recruit than the womanizing crooner he'd admired since he was seven. Together we probably looked like the founding members of a Vin Diesel fan club.

"Nice," he said, checking out the new do in a hand mirror. "My head feels ten pounds lighter."

"It's really white. You need to self-tan your scalp or something."

"Oh, hush," he said. "You're just jealous because I look so much better than you do bald." He scrambled to his feet. "I hear fireworks. Want to go see?"

"Sure."

It was dark outside, and the fireflies twinkled gold against the asphalt. When I was little I'd thought that fireflies were fairies. I thought if I caught one and held on to it long enough, it would turn into Tinker Bell and make me fly.

"Pretty," I murmured.

"Yeah," he said, but he wasn't looking at the lightning bugs.

I pretended not to notice his stare. "I don't see any fireworks."

"You can hear them, though, if you listen hard."

Sure enough, I heard the low, faraway booms. It made me sad, not being able to see them. I couldn't remember the last time we'd missed the big display. Even before the Riverfront had opened, we'd always made the trek to Rockford Park. I still had all the glow necklaces I'd collected over the years, though they'd long since lost their juice.

"What are you thinking about?" Critter asked.

"I'm thinking," I said, "that it's been a hell of a summer so far."

"No doubt," he agreed. Then he groaned. "I can't believe our vacation is already over."

The thing was, I was actually looking forward to starting class. For the first time in my life, I craved routine. That and the chance to finally prove not just to Layla or even Jesse, but to *me* as well—that I was really capable of more.

Critter, though—he just looked so . . . deflated. "It won't be that bad," I said, ruffling his nonexistent hair. "Summer school will be over before you know it. And then we'll hang out for the rest of August like we always do."

He chuckled softly. "Sure."

I looked down and noticed that the edges of one of my scabs—from my big lipslide wipeout—had started to curl. I picked at the loose flakes and sighed. "What do you want me to say?"

Right then, an enormous explosion of color lit up the sky. Swirling tendrils of red, purple, and green streaked through the darkness, followed by electric spiderwebs of white.

"Whoa," Critter said, his head popping up. "Did you see that?"

I didn't have time to respond, but he wouldn't have heard me anyway. There were more explosions, big and loud and bright, followed by the ones that shriek as they burn. The neighbors started spilling out of their houses to watch the show, and it wasn't long before Layla and Jesse came outside to join us.

The whole thing lasted maybe six minutes, but it was long enough for me. Critter, too, if the carefree smile he was wearing was any indication. The four of us were squeezed on the stoop, Layla to my right and Jesse to Critter's left, and after the crap we'd all been dealing with, it felt really good to just sit there with them— my family.

"Hey, rock star," I whispered in Critter's ear. "Love ya."

He nudged my shoulder gently. "Yeah," he said, still smiling. "Me too."

About the Author

lara m. zeises is the author of two other novels for young adults, *Bringing Up the Bones,* a Delacorte Press Prize Honor Book, and *Contents Under Pressure,* which began as her thesis project at Emerson College, where she earned her MFA in creative writing. She is the recipient of an Emerging Artist Fellowship in Literature—Fiction from the Delaware Division of the Arts.

Lara has never ridden a skateboard or worshipped at the altar of Rod Stewart, but she does share her characters' deep-seated appreciation for air-conditioning. She lives in Delaware, where she grew up, but you can visit her on the Web at www.zeisgeist.com.